RICARDO GÜIRALDES
was one of the initiators of
the post-World War I literary
movement in Argentina. He was born in February
1886, into a family of the old landowning aristocracy.
At the age of two the baby Ricardo was taken to
Europe; when he returned, four years later, he spoke
French and German as fluently as Spanish. His boyhood was spent between the family's city home in
Buenos Aires and the ranch, La Porteña, at San
Antonio de Areco. The author studied law but never
practiced. He traveled extensively in Europe, but he
always returned to his beloved Argentina, where he
applied the intellectual and artistic training that he
won from the Old World to the expression of the life
of his own land. He was a cofounder of the literary
reviews *Martín Fierro* and *Proa,* in which the early
work of many of the young writers who later achieved
distinction first appeared. His first work was a volume
of poems, *El Concerro de cristal,* published in 1915;
but it is as a novelist and short-story writer that he
achieved his greatest fame. His first volume of short
stories, *Cuentos de muerte y de sangre,* also appeared
in 1915. These were followed in 1917 by the novels
Rosaura and *Raucho.* In 1923 he published *Xaimaca,*
the sentimental diary of a traveler who visits many
countries in the company of a mysterious woman.
Three years later he completed *Don Segundo Sombra,*
his consummate work of art. Ricardo Güiraldes died
on October 8, 1927, in Paris, France.

Don Segundo Sombra

SHADOWS ON THE PAMPAS

by Ricardo Güiraldes

Translated and with an Afterword by
Harriet de Onís

Illustrated by
Alberto Güiraldes

A SIGNET CLASSIC Published by
THE NEW AMERICAN LIBRARY, NEW YORK AND TORONTO
THE NEW ENGLISH LIBRARY LIMITED, LONDON

Published as a SIGNET CLASSIC by arrangement with
Holt, Rinehart & Winston, Inc., who have authorized
this softcover edition.

First Printing, January, 1966

SIGNET TRADEMARK REG. U.S. PAT. OFF. AND FOREIGN COUNTRIES
REGISTERED TRADEMARK—MARCA REGISTRADA
HECHO EN CHICAGO, U.S.A.

SIGNET CLASSICS are published *in the United States* by
The New American Library, Inc.,
1301 Avenue of the Americas, New York, New York 10019,
in Canada by The New American Library of Canada Limited,
295 King Street East, Toronto 2, Ontario,
in the United Kingdom by The New English Library Limited,
Barnard's Inn, Holborn, London, E.C. 1, England

PRINTED IN THE UNITED STATES OF AMERICA

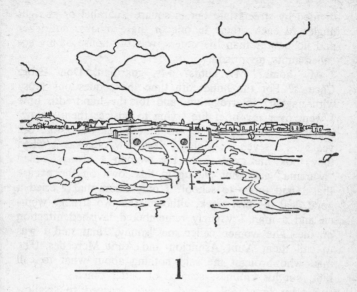

1

On the outskirts of the town, some ten blocks from the main square, the old bridge throws its arch across the river, linking the houses and gardens to the placid countryside.

That day, as usual, I had come to hide in the cool shade of the rocks and hook a few catfish, which I would later trade to the storekeeper at La Blanqueada for candy, cigarettes, or cash. But I was not in my usual good spirits: I felt strangely sullen and unsociable, and had not rounded up the gang that loafed and fished with me, because I did not feel like smiling or repeating the customary wisecracks. Even fishing seemed a superfluous gesture, and I let my float drift with the current and come to rest against the bank.

I was thinking . . . thinking of my fourteen years as a *guacho*—the name everyone around there surely gave me—an abandoned orphan. With eyes half shut to keep out the things I did not want to see, I pictured the town's forty blocks, the low flat houses monotonously divided by streets laid out in squares, parallel or at right angles to each other. In one of these blocks, no richer and no poorer than the others, was the house of my so-called aunts, my prison.

My home? My aunts? My guardian, Don Fabio Cáceres? For the hundredth time those questions arose with nagging interrogation, and for the hundredth time I went over my brief life trying to answer them, knowing it was useless; but it was a stubborn obsession. Six years . . . seven . . . eight? Just how old was I when they took me away from the woman I always called "Mamma" and shut me up in this town on the excuse that I had to go to school? I only know that I cried a good deal the first week, although the two strange women and a man I vaguely remembered lavished affection on me. The women called me "sonny," and said I was to call them Aunt Asunción and Aunt Mercedes. The man who brought me said nothing about what to call him, but his kindness seemed of better omen.

I went to school. I had already learned to swallow my tears and to mistrust sweet words. My aunts soon tired of their new toy and scolded all day long. The only thing they agreed on was that I was a lazy, dirty good-for-nothing and that I was to blame for everything that went amiss in the house.

Don Fabio Cáceres came for me once and asked if I'd care to visit his ranch. I got to know his fine house, which was far better than any other in this whole town; it awed me into respectful silence like the church where my aunts took me and stuck me between them so they could prompt me with my beads and watch every move I made as though each glare and thump meant a star in their crown. Don Fabio showed me the barnyard, gave me a cookie and a peach, and drove me around in his sulky to see the cows and the mares. Back in town, the memory of that visit was a bright spot in my life, and when I thought of it, I couldn't keep from crying because it brought back, somehow, the farm where I was born and the shadowy figure of Mamma forever busy with some chore while I hung around the kitchen or splashed in a puddle.

Don Fabio came for me two or three times more, and that was the end of the first year. By then my aunts paid no attention to me except on Sundays, when they dragged me to Mass, and at night, when they made me say the rosary. On both occasions I was like a prisoner between two policemen who gradually economized on reprimands by turning them into slaps.

For three years I went to school; I don't remember what set me free. One day my aunts announced that it wasn't worthwhile trying to give me an education; and after that I was sent on a thousand and one errands that kept me continually in the street.

The folks I met in the saloon, the store, the post office, were good to me; they smiled and asked nothing. The joy and warmth hidden in my heart burst its deep dungeon and my real nature bubbled forth, free, colorful, gay. The street was my paradise, the house my torture chamber; the more friends I made outside, the more I hated my aunts. I became bold. I did not hesitate to walk right into the hotel and chat with the bigwigs who gathered there mornings and afternoons for a game of cards. I hung around the barbershop, where you learn all the latest news, and I soon came to know people as well as things. Not a joke or a smart comeback but stuck in my head; I became a kind of grab bag in which folks liked to stir about with their teasing until I let out some rare scorcher.

I knew the details of the town marshal's affair with the widow Eulalia, all about the rackets of the Gambuttis, and the shady reputation of Porro, the watchmaker. One day Gómez, the saloonkeeper, egged me on to say *"retarjo"* to the postman Moreira, who came back at me with *"guacho,"* and that made me suspect for the first time that there was some sort of mystery about me that nobody wanted to reveal. But I was too happy at having achieved popularity and admiration in the street to let anything disturb me. These were the happiest days of my childhood.

My aunts' indifference encountered even greater indifference on my part, and the brashness I had developed in my life as a street urchin made it easier for me
to endure their nagging. I even went so far as to slip out
at night, and one Sunday I went to the races, where a
rumpus took place, and some shooting, but nobody was
hurt.

With all this I soon came to think I was a grown man;
and, in all good faith, I treated the other kids my own
age as if they were two-year-olds. I got to be known
as a smart aleck, and I lived up to my fame, glutting
with the cruel ignorance of a child the wicked will of
the strong over the weak.

"Go take a dig at Juan Sosa," someone would suggest; "he's there at the bar stewed to the gills."

Four or five who were in on the joke clustered at
the door or sat at nearby tables to listen, while I, puffed
up by vanity, walked over to Sosa and held out my
hand.

"How goes it, Juan?"

". . ."

"Lord, you're drunk. You don't even know who I
am!"

The souse squinted at me as over a distance of a century. He knew me well enough but kept quiet, suspect-
ing a trick.

I came closer and, swelling out my body and voice
like a toad, said, "Can't you see I'm your wife, Filomena?
Just you keep up this guzzling and when you get home
tonight I'm going to duck you arse-first in the pond till
you're over your jag."

Juan Sosa raised his hand to slap me, but the laughter
from the other tables made me bold.

I did not budge and went on sternly, "Don't you dare
threaten me, Juan. Your hand might slip and break a
glass. Remember the marshal doesn't like drunks; he'll
fan your ribs like he did the last time. Have you forgotten about it?"

Poor Sosa turned his hunted eyes on the hotel owner,
who winked at the fellows who had brought me in.

"Boss," he pleaded, "tell this snotnose to get out of here. He might make me lose my temper."

The owner made believe he was angry and shouted, "Come on, kid. Beat it now, and let folks alone."

Once outside with the others, I claimed my pay. "And now where's my peso?"

"A peso? You must have caught Sosa's jag from him."

"Oh, come on. Give me a peso and I'll show you something."

With a smile the man handed the money over, looking for some new bit of clowning, and he wasn't cheated.

"Come on, boys," I said to him and the others in a patronizing tone, "the drinks are on me. Let's have a beer." And right there, in the hotel, I ordered the bottles myself and set up the drinks, telling them, meanwhile, what I had learned about Melo's racing sorrel and the fight between the half-breed Burgos and Sinforiano Herrera, and how the dirty gringo Culasso had sold his twelve-year-old daughter to old Salomovich, the whorehouse owner, for twenty pesos.

There were comments on my reputation as a know-it-all and wise guy of which I was not aware at the time. The decent people called me a limb of Satan and predicted that I would come to a bad end. This made certain folks eye me askance; but, on the other hand, it put me in right with the town rowdies. They stood me drinks at the saloons—brandy and punch to get me befuddled—but a certain natural wariness kept me safe from their wiles. One night Pencho swung me behind him on his pony and took me to the brothel. Only after I got inside did I know where I was, but I bluffed it through and nobody noticed how scared I was.

Being in the limelight is a thrill for a while; then you get tired of it. Life soon became a bore again, no matter how much I hung around the hotel, the barbershop, the general store, La Blanqueada, where the owner made a fuss over me and I met "outsiders": herders, strangers, or hands from the nearby ranches. Luckily for me, about this time, when I was twelve, Don Fabio proved more the kind guardian than ever. He came to see me

often, either to take me with him to the ranch or to
bring me some present. He gave me a little poncho,
and a new suit of clothes, and even—the best of all—a
pair of ponies and a saddle so I could ride with him
on our excursions.

This went on for a year, but it was written in my
stars that my good luck was not to last. All of a sudden
Don Fabio stopped coming. As for my ponies, my aunts
loaned one of them to Festal, the son of the storekeeper, whom I hated because he was stuck-up and a
sissy. The saddle was stuck away in the attic on the excuse that I had no use for it.

I was lonelier than ever. Folks had begun to get tired
of amusing themselves with me, and besides I no longer
tried to entertain them.

Now my life as a young vagabond led me to the river.
There I found new friends: the miller's son, Manzoni,
and a Negro boy, Lechuza, who was already deaf from
too much swimming underwater, though he was only fifteen. I learned to swim, and I went fishing every day
because it was a way of earning a penny.

Gradually my memories had brought me back to the
present. I found myself thinking again how wonderful it
would be to get away, but even this thought faded into
the afternoon whose silence the twilight was beginning
to drape in its early shadows. The mud of the bank and
the gullies turned violet. The rough bed rocks gleamed like
metal. The waters of the river turned cold as I watched,
and the reflections of things on the quiet surface had
more color than the things themselves. The sky receded.
The gold tints of the clouds turned red, the red, dun.

I picked up my string of "tough-to-kill" catfish, still
writhing in the agony of slow asphyxiation; I wrapped
my line around the pole, stuck the hook in the cork, and
turned toward town, where the first lights were beginning to wink.

Above the low, sprawled houses the night was thrusting into eminence the old belfry of the church.

2

Slowly, with my fishing rod over my shoulder and dangling my small victims heartlessly at my side, I made my way toward town. The street still was flooded by a recent thundershower, and I had to walk carefully to keep from sinking in the mud that clung to my sandals and almost sucked them off my feet. My mind was a blank as I took the narrow path that crept along the hedges of prickly pear, thorn, myrrh, following the rise of the ground, like hares seeking a level place to run.

The lane ahead of me stretched dark. The sky, still blue with twilight, lay in reflected shards in the puddles or in the deep wagon ruts, where it looked like strips of carefully trimmed steel.

I had reached the first houses, where the hour put the dogs on the alert. Fear twitched in my legs as I heard the growl of a dangerous mastiff not far off, but without a mistake I called all the brutes by name: Sentinel, Captain, Watcher. When some mutt set up a barking as swift as it was inoffensive, I disdainfully shied a clod at it.

I passed the graveyard and a familiar tremor ran down my spine, radiating its pallid chill to my calves and forearms. The dead, will-o'-the-wisps, ghosts, scared me far more than any encounter I might have with mortals in that neighborhood. What could the greediest robber hope for from me? I was on good terms with the slyest of them; and if one was so careless as to hold me up, he would be the loser by a cigarette.

The lane became a street, the outlying farms thickened into blocks of houses; and neither walls nor bead-tree hedges held any secrets for me. Here was a stand of alfalfa, there a patch of corn, a barn lot, or just brush. Now I could make out the first shanties, silent in their squalor and illumined only by the frail glow of a candle or stinking kerosene lamps. As I crossed a street I frightened a horse whose step had sounded farther off than it was; and as fear is catching, even from animal to man, I stood stock-still in the mud without daring to move. The rider, who seemed to me enormous in his light poncho, urged the horse on, whirling the whiplash past its left eye; but as soon as I tried to take a step the scared beast snorted like a mule and reared. A puddle cracked beneath his hoof with the sound of breaking glass. A high-pitched voice spoke calmly, "Steady, boy. Steady, boy."

Then trot and gallop splashed through the sleek mud.

I stood still and watched the silhouette of horse and rider disappear strangely magnified against the glowing sky. It was as if I had seen a vision, a shade, a something that passes and is more a thought than a living thing, a something that drew me as a pool swallows the current of a river into its depths.

Filled with my vision, I reached the first sidewalks, where I could make better time. Stronger than ever was the need I felt to get away, to leave this paltry town forever. I had glimpsed a new life, a life of motion and space.

In a whirl of dreams and doubts I kept on through the

town and down the blackness of another alley to La Blanqueada. As I entered, the light made me pucker up my eyes. Behind the counter, as usual, stood the owner, and in front of him the half-breed Burgos was just finishing off a brandy.

"Good evening, gentlemen."

"Evening," mumbled Burgos.

"What you got?" asked the owner.

"There you are, Don Pedro." I showed him my string of catfish.

"All right. Want some rock candy?"

"No, Don Pedro."

"Couple packages of La Popular?"

"No, Don Pedro. Remember the last money you gave me?"

"Sure."

"It was round."

"And you made it roll?"

"You said it."

"All right. Here you are." He clinked several nickel coins down on the counter.

"Gonna set up the drinks?" grinned the half-breed.

"Sure—in the *Wouldn't You Like It* café."

"Anything new?" asked Don Pedro, for whom I was a kind of reporter.

"Yes, sir; a stranger."

"Where'd you see him?"

"At the crossing, as I was coming in from the river."

"And you don't know who he is?"

"I know he's not from here. There's no man as big as him in this town."

Don Pedro frowned, as if trying to concentrate on some half-forgotten memory. "Tell me, was he very dark?"

"I think so—yes, sir. And strong!"

As though talking of something extraordinary, the saloonkeeper muttered, "Who knows if it isn't Don Segundo Sombra!"

"It is!" I said, without knowing why, and I felt the same thrill as when at nightfall I had stood motionless before the portentous vision of that gaucho stamped black on the horizon.

"You know him?" Don Pedro asked the half-breed, paying no attention to my exclamation.

"Only what I've heard tell of him. The devil, I reckon, ain't as fierce as he's painted. How about serving me another drink?"

"Hm," went on Don Pedro. "I've seen him more than once. He used to come in here, afternoons. He's a man you want to watch your step with. He's from San Pedro. Had a run in, they say, with the police some time ago."

"I suppose he butchered somebody else's steer."

"Yes. But, if I remember rightly, the steer was a Christian."

Burgos kept his stolid eyes on the glass, and a frown wrinkled his narrow forehead of a pampas Indian half-breed. The fame of another man seemed to lessen his own as an expert with the knife.

We heard a gallop stop short at the door, then the soft hiss with which the country folk quiet a horse, and Don Segundo's silent figure stood framed in the doorway.

"Good evening," came the high-pitched voice, and it was easy to recognize. "How's Don Pedro?"

"Good. And you, Don Segundo?"

"I can't complain, thank God."

As they greeted each other with the customary courtesies, I looked the man over. He was not really so big. What made him seem so, as he appears to me even today, was the sense of power flowing from his body. His chest was enormous and his joints big-boned like those of a horse. His feet were short and high-arched; his hands thick and leathery like the scales of an armadillo. His skin was copper-hued and his eyes slanted slightly toward his temples. To talk more at ease he pushed his narrow-brimmed hat back from his forehead showing bangs cut like a horse's, level with his eyebrows. His attire was that of a poor gaucho. A plain pigskin belt girded his waist. The short blouse was caught up by the bone-handled knife from which swung a rough, plaited quirt, dark with use. His *chiripá* was long and coarse, and a plain black kerchief was knotted around his neck with the ends across his shoulders. He had split his *alpargatas* at the instep to make room for the fleshy foot.

When I had looked my fill at him, I listened to the talk. Don Segundo was looking for work, and Don Pedro was telling him where to find it; his constant business with the country people made him know everything that was going on at the ranches.

"At Galván's there are some mares they want broke. A few days ago Valerio was here and asked me if there was anyone I could recommend. I told him about Mosco Pereira, but if it suits you—"

"Seems to me it might."

"Good. I'll tell the boy they send to town every day. He generally drops in."

"I'd rather you said nothing. If I can, I'll go by the ranch myself."

"All right. Like a drink?"

"Well, I don't mind," said Don Segundo, sitting down at a nearby table. "Give me a glass of brandy, and thanks for the invitation."

Everything that had to be said was said. A calm silence filled the place. Burgos poured out his fourth glass. His eyes were bleary and his face expressionless. Suddenly, and for no apparent reason, he said to me, "If I was a fisher like you, I'd want to haul in a great big mud-bottom catfish." A sarcastic giggle underlined his words, and he kept looking at Don Segundo out of the corner of his eye. "They seem tough because they flop around and make such a fuss. But what can they do when they're nothing but niggers."

Don Pedro gave the half-breed a sharp look. Both of us knew what Burgos was like and that nothing could hold him when he turned ugly. The only one of the four of us who didn't understand the drift of things was Don Segundo, who went on sipping his liquor, his thoughts far away. The half-breed giggled again; he was proud of the comparison he had hit on. I longed to do something —something terrible if need be—to break the strain.

Don Pedro was humming to himself. And the air was
tense for us all, except for the stranger, who seemed to
have neither understood nor felt the chill of our silence.

"A big mud-bottom catfish," repeated the drunk again.
"But nothing but a catfish, for all it's got whiskers and
walks on two legs like Christians. . . . I've heard there's
a lot of 'em in San Pedro. That's why they say:

> 'Anyone from San Pedro
> Is either a chink or a mulatto.' "

Twice he repeated the rhyme in a voice that grew
thicker and more insolent.

Don Segundo looked up and, as if just realizing that
the half-breed's words were meant for him, said calmly, "Come, friend, I'll soon begin to think you're trying
to start something."

So unexpected were the words, so amusing the expression of surprise on his face, that we had to smile despite
the ugly turn the talk was taking. The drunk himself was
nonplussed, but only for a moment.

"Yeah? I was beginning to think everybody around
here was deaf."

"How could a catfish be deaf, with the big ears they
got? But me? I'm a busy man and I can't take care of
you now. When you want to fight with me, let me know
at least three days in advance."

We burst out laughing, in spite of the amazement this
calm that verged on foolhardiness aroused in us. Again
he began to grow in my imagination. He was the
"masked man," the "mystery man," the man of silence,
who inspires a wondering admiration in the pampas.

The half-breed Burgos paid for his drinks, muttering
threats. I followed him to the door and saw him hide
in the shadow. Don Segundo got up and took his leave
of Don Pedro, who was pale with fear. The drunk was
going to kill this man to whom my heart went out! As
if speaking to Don Pedro, I warned Don Segundo:
"Watch out!"

And then I sat down on the doorsill, my heart in my mouth, waiting for the fight that was sure to come.

Don Segundo stood on the threshold, looking from side to side. I understood that he was getting his eyes used to the dark, so as not to be taken by surprise. Then, keeping to the wall, he started toward his horse.

The half-breed stepped from the shadow feeling sure of his man and let loose his knife aimed straight at the heart. I saw the blade cut the night like the flash of a gun. With incredible swiftness Don Segundo dodged, and the knife shattered against the brick wall with the clang of a bell. Burgos stepped back two paces and waited for what must be his death. The triangular blade of a small knife glittered in Don Segundo's fist. But the attack did not come. Don Segundo bent calmly over, picked the broken steel from the ground, and said in his ironic voice, "Here you are, friend. Better get it fixed. This way, it's no good even to skin a sheep."

The attacker kept his distance. Don Segundo put away his own little knife and again held out the fragments of the blade.

"Take it, friend."

The bully came forward, his head low, moved by a force stronger than his fear. His clumsy fist took the hilt of the knife, now harmless as a broken cross. Don Segundo shrugged and walked toward his horse. And Burgos followed him. Don Segundo mounted and made ready to move into the night. The drunk came close, seeming to have recovered the gift of speech.

"Listen, friend," he said and raised his sullen face, in which only the eyes were alive. "I'm gonna have this knife fixed for whenever you need me." The dull bully's mind could think of only one act of thanks: to offer his life to the other. "Now, shake."

"Sure thing," agreed Don Segundo, as calm as ever. "Put it there, brother."

And without further ado he went down the narrow street, while the half-breed stood seeming to struggle with a thought too great and radiant for him.

I went striding along beside Don Segundo, who kept his horse at a walk.

"You know that fellow?" he asked, muffling himself in his voluminous poncho with a leisurely gesture.

"Yes, sir. I know him well."

"Seems sort of foolish, don't he?"

3

In front of my house Don Segundo shook my hand, then went on toward the inn where he was going to eat. That handshake, I guessed, was his thanks for my warning as he left La Blanqueada; and I felt very proud.

I walked into the house, taking my time. It was late, and as I expected, my aunts gave me a tongue lashing, called me a good-for-nothing, and condemned me to bed without supper. I looked at them as one looks at an old whip that's no longer of any use. Aunt Mercedes, sharp and skinny, with a hawk's nose jutting between her sunken eyes, was the one who decided I should get nothing to eat. Aunt Asunción, paunchy, loose breasted, greedy for every pleasure, did most of the scolding. I told them where to get off and locked myself in my room to think over my future and to digest the day's event. My life, it seemed to me, was bound to Don Segundo's; and though I saw the thousand and thousand stumbling blocks to it, I had the secret hope that it would all work out. The question was, how?

First I thought it might happen this way: Don Segundo would again get into trouble and I, a second time, would warn him. This would happen three or four times, and finally the man would have to accept me as his mascot. Or it would be because we discovered that we were distantly related, and he would become my guardian. As a last resort, it might be that he simply took a liking to me and let me live at his side, half servant, half waif. For the moment, at any rate, I knew what to do. Don Segundo was going to the Galváns'? Well, I'd get there first. Having got this far in my thoughts, I stopped. The immediate solution was good enough, and besides, it doesn't help to go on thinking until you're worn out.

"I'm going, I'm going," I said half aloud. I sat on the bed in the dark, so that my aunts would think me asleep, and waited for the propitious moment to take off. The last noises, proclaiming the stupidity of my daily world, wore themselves away, and the house dozed. Already the paltry life I'd been living was unbearable to me, and in a rage I stared at the blank walls of my room as one might look without mercy at a beaten foe. Nothing there that I would miss, for the bridle and halter that I could dimly make out on a nail against the door were going with me. These walls that had looked unmoved on my first tears, on my loneliness, on my rebellions—good riddance to them!

I groped under the bed for a pair of well-worn boots; alongside them I laid the bridle and halter; and on top I threw my beloved poncho, Don Fabio's gift, and my few changes of clothing. My courage gathered as I made my preparations. I slipped cautiously into the backyard, leaving the door open. The immensity of the night frightened me, as though it had learned my secret. I made my way to the loft. The dog Sergeant was glad to see me. I climbed the narrow stair to the vast room where the mice scampered among the few sacks of corn and discarded furniture.

It was hard to find the scattered parts of my saddle, but luckily I had a box of matches in my pocket, and the fitful little flame helped me gather up the saddle-cloth, leather pad, cushions, sheepskin, leather, and cinch. I fastened them with the cinch strap, threw the bundle across my shoulder, and returned to my room, where I added these new possessions to my poncho, boots, and bridle. As there was nothing more to take away, I threw myself down on the floor in the midst of my belongings, leaving the bed untouched, feeling thereby that I was cutting myself free from the shackles of the past.

It was still night when I awoke. My right flank ached from resting on the bit, my backside was cold from the brick floor, and my neck was stiff. What time was it? At any rate the sensible thing was to be ready for whatever might happen. I made a single bundle of my clothes and saddle outfit, threw the lot over my shoulder like a peddler's pack, and still half asleep, felt my way to the barn lot. I bridled and saddled my pony, threw open the large gate, and rode into the street. I felt a satisfaction I had never known before, the satisfaction of being free.

The town still slept grimly. I rode my pony at a walk, which the silent streets made strangely sonorous, toward the Torres livery stable. There the Festal boy kept my other pony, and I was going to get it. A cock crowed. Vaguely day dawned. They have to get up early at the stable, to meet the morning train, and I found the door open. Remigio, one of my friends among the bigger boys, was with the horses.

"Where'd you blow in from?" was his first question.

"Good morning, brother. I've come for my pony."

I had to argue a lot with the stubborn fool to convince him I had a right to my own belongings. At last he shrugged his shoulders.

"Well, there he is. Do whatever you like."

I didn't wait for a second invitation. I bridled the animal, which, I must confess, was in better shape than the one I had cared for. I said good-bye to Remigio. And like a regular gaucho, with my worldly goods on my back and my second horse behind me, I set out over the old bridge toward the country.

To get to Galván's place you set out the same way

as to Don Fabio's. Then at a certain spot a lane turns off to the north and leads to a small wood that I had long known from afar. I was so eager to get away from the town that I set off at a gallop, and my second pony led perfectly. After traveling two leagues I stopped to let the animals blow as the sun rose over my new life!

I was immersed in an unutterable well-being. A new day drenched the countryside with gold and enameled my ponies with fresh color. The meadows all around came silently to life again, glittering with dew; and I laughed with a great gladness, I laughed from freedom, while my eyes filled with crystals as if they too had been reborn in the dew of the new morning.

I still had a league to go to reach the houses, and I covered it at a fast canter, while the young day sang about me, filling me with faith in a dawn that seemed, as it scattered the night, to be giving birth to the pampa.

I was nervous about going straight up to the main house, so I turned toward the stables. There didn't seem to be a soul around. The dogs that growled and snapped at my ponies' heels were not exactly an invitation to dismount. At last an old fellow stuck his head out the kitchen door, yelled "Get out!" to the pack, told me to come in, and motioned me to have a seat on one of the many stools around the room.

All morning long I stayed in that corner and watched every move the old man made, as if my future depended on it. We didn't speak a word.

At noon the farmhands began to straggle in, and the dinner bell sounded. As the men entered, they nodded to me, and a few gave me a sidelong glance. Goyo López, whom I knew from town, came in with four or five others.

"Just ridin' around?" he asked me.

"I'm looking for work."

"Work?" he repeated and gave me a sharp look. A chill ran over me, for I thought he was going to say something about my family in town. But Goyo was a discreet fellow. The men were watching me. At last a burly lad said, "I s'pose he can carry the sacks of grain."

"Go ahead." Goyo turned toward him. "Ride him now,

while he's green. 'Cause after he's been here awhile he may be ridin' you. You don't know this bronc."

I was the center of forty eyes. I didn't even blink, waiting for the interest to wane. But Goyo's words had had their effect. To be wide-awake, even beyond the limits of good behavior, is a virtue in the eyes of the country folk. Goyo called to me from the door to come and unsaddle my pony; he would show me the watering trough, he said. And this, of course, was a move to get me away where he could talk to me alone.

"You've run away from town," he said at once.

"Please, pal, don't say anything. You'll get me in trouble."

"I get you in trouble? Fat chance. What are you going to do? Work?"

"And why not?"

"All right, then. Water the horse. Look. Here comes the overseer."

We waited for the gone-native Britisher to come our way. I bowed and asked for a job.

"Haven't any," he said and slipped off his horse.

"May I stay, then, and have some chow? I'll leave right after."

"Where to?"

"Over there," I answered, pointing vaguely.

The Englishman smiled at me.

"Do you mind well?"

"Yes, sir."

"Do you know him, Goyo?"

"A little, Don Jeremiah."

"All right. After siesta, let him hitch Frog to the cart and carry the litter from the stalls to the ditches near the white gate."

"Yes, sir."

To get on the right side of the boss, I ran to his horse, unsaddled it, turned the pad so it would dry out, and asked Goyo where I should take it.

"To that corral there with the barley."

The Englishman watched me with a smile as I led his horse to the trough.

"With or without bridle?" I asked Goyo.

"Without."

I can't tell you my happiness as I sat down at the long table already flanked by twenty men, taking my place between Goyo and an old gringo who had charge of the garden.

"Cook!" yelled Goyo. "Give the new hand a plate and spoon."

"New hand?" laughed the boy who had already made fun of me when I said I was looking for work. "What's he gonna do? Haul manure?"

I realized that those words, which in someone else would have been an insult, were only stupidity on his part, and I decided to take advantage of them to make good Goyo's boast about me.

"Haul manure?" I repeated. "You'd better watch out you don't wake up some morning on a pile of it yourself."

The round of laughter made me think of the days of my popularity in town.

"You've got a mean disposition," I went on, my eyes on the kinky and tousled head of my rival; "if I was the boss, I'd have that wool cut off to stuff horse collars with."

There was a general guffaw. When it died down, one of the older men came back to me, "You seem to know a lot. But it's not a good thing to try to fly before your wings have sprouted. You're still too much of a pup to be pissing like a dog."

One glance was enough to show me who was talking, and I lowered my head and answered, gently, as one should when talking to an older person, "Don't you believe it, sir. I know how to be respectful, too."

"I'm glad to hear it," the old man closed the episode. After a brief pause, good feeling was back at the table.

I spent the whole afternoon hauling the dirty straw from the stalls to the ditches about half a mile away. At the barn a stableman loaded my wagon, leaving the pitchfork stuck in the manure. At the ditches I unloaded, and on the way back the pitchfork rattled on the floor of the cart fit to raise the dead. By suppertime I could hardly keep my eyes open, but in the general silence my weariness, which I feared would make me the butt of jokes, passed unnoticed.

They put up a cot for me in Goyo's room. I had neither mattress nor cover to soften the inhospitable bed, but weariness is the best featherbed. I wrapped my poncho around me and lay down on the bare canvas without worrying about refinements. For a moment I thought of my escapade; I recalled the house of my aunts, their faces, the prayers they had made me say. Sleep fell over me like a straw stack on a sparrow.

4

Horacio shook me by the shoulders till I woke up. My first thought was of the day before: flight, the success of my scheme to get to Galván's ranch ahead of Don Segundo, Goyo's welcome, my introduction to the men as a new hand, the incident at the table. It was just getting light; through the small window I could see the clouds in the east coming alive with gold, like long and delicate sunflower petals. I got my feet off the cot and painfully onto the floor; my legs were soft as cheese. I cinched in my belt, rubbed my eyes (heavy as if hornets had stung them), and shuffled my way to the kitchen. I was cold and I ached all over.

The men were just finishing their maté, grouped around the already-ashen hearth. I gulped three bitter ones, one after the other, and that helped wake me up. "Let's go," said someone, and as if we had been waiting for that signal, we all scattered through the door in different directions.

The first glance of the sun found me sweeping out the

sheepfolds with a big palm-leaf broom. Not a very proud occupation, perhaps, that of brushing the droppings from the brick floor and gathering stray strands of greasy wool; but I was happy as morning. I did my job with care, telling myself that thanks to it I was like the grown men. The cool of the morning roused me. In the sky the colors faded, overpowered by the daylight.

At eight we were called to breakfast, and as I chewed my hunk of barbecued meat I studied my comrades, trying to learn all I could from their faces. The head wrangler, Valerio Lares, was a brawny half-breed, close-mouthed but pleasant; I wanted to make friends with him, but I didn't want to be too forward. Besides, nobody talked; the little time we had was put to better use. When breakfast was over, the cook told me to stay and help him; all the others gradually went off, leaving the big room empty. The huge hearth was its heart; under the hood was a big kettle and surrounding it the little maté gourds squatting like chicks around the mother ostrich. The cook was no more talkative than on the day I came, and I spent a silent morning doing odd jobs in the kitchen. My eyes kept straying to the door, where the wrangler sat in silent silhouette, sewing a pair of raw-hide reins.

It must have been close to noon when we heard a rattle of spurs on the bricks outside. Valerio was greeting someone and inviting him to have a maté. I peered out, and there was Don Segundo Sombra.

"Just riding past?" asked Valerio.

"No, sir. I heard you had some mares to be broke, and that you were mighty busy."

"Won't you come into the kitchen?"

"All right."

The two men came up to the hearth. Don Segundo said good day to me as though he did not recognize me. They took low stools by the fire, and the talk began, broken by long pauses.

"Hey, boy," Valerio turned to order me, "get a gourd and brew a maté for Don Segundo."

"This one?"

"No, not that one. That's Gualberto's and he's fussy about his things. There's one on the table."

Delighted, I put the kettle on the embers, poked up the flame, filled the gourd from the canister.

"Sweet or bitter?"

"Any way."

"Sweet then."

"All right."

I drew up a stool for myself, and while the water bubbled I cast a reproachful eye on Don Segundo because he had not greeted me more warmly. Neither man spoke, so at last I ventured to ask, "Don't you remember me?"

Don Segundo looked right through me, taking no notice of me.

"I'm the one," I went on, "that scared your horse night before last, just outside of town."

I expected some sign of recognition, but instead he looked me over curiously, as though expecting to find something odd about my face.

"Your tongue," he said, "sort of hangs in the middle and swings at both ends."

I understood, and the blood rushed to my cheeks. Don Segundo was afraid I might give myself away and preferred not to know me. For a long while we sat in silence; then the slow talk between the wrangler and the newcomer began again.

"There a lot of the mares?"

"No, sir. Just eight."

"I've heard tell this breed can't stand much cinching."

"No, they're just a little cranky, that's all."

The bell rang for the noonday meal. Don Segundo kept sucking at his sipper, and twice I changed the maté leaves. Now the men were coming in, heavy with the heat but happy at a respite from work. They all knew the stranger, and the room was filled for a time with greetings. But a ranch does not stay quiet long. Goyo tripped over Horacio's feet, who threw a saddle pad at his head. The men formed a ring around the two, who were in the habit of pummeling each other at every opportunity.

"Bet I can black your face, you bum," shouted Horacio, and the two went over to the hearth and smeared their fingers on the bottom of the pot. Then, with legs spread, left arm forward as though protected by a poncho, and right circling in quick feints, they tried to mark each other's face with soot. The scrimmage ended when Horacio put up the ends of his neckcloth to hide the mark on his cheek.

"You're hard to take," said Goyo.

"Is that what your sister said?"

"Say, where do you get off—"

A real fight threatened, but the arrival of the owner put a stop to it. He was a man with a gruff air. Don Segundo walked over to him and explained his business. They stepped outside to talk it over, and the kitchen was as quiet as Mass.

Don Segundo ate with us and told us it was all fixed up for him to start breaking the mares that afternoon. Valerio arranged to drive them to the corral toward sundown, so they wouldn't suffer too much.

"If you need hobbles, bridles, or anything, just sing out and I'll be glad to lend them to you."

"Thanks. I think I've got everything."

Dog-tired though I was, I couldn't sleep that siesta,

trying to figure out a way to be present at the breaking. I knew that the owner had urged Don Segundo to be careful because of his weight; but who can keep a bronco from bucking? When the time came I managed to be hauling loads of broken wire, scrap iron, and smashed fence posts out to the ditches. And on the way I could cross the field and perhaps get at least a glimpse of the work.

Things developed as I had foreseen. The first three mares were gentle; the only trouble they gave was to the men who led them out. The fourth tried to shake off the weight on her back, but the wrangler's powerful hands were too much for her, preventing her from getting her head down. The fifth was another breed of cat. Don Segundo wouldn't let her run, so she bucked furious-

ly, whirling around and around in the meanest, most dangerous manner.

By a lucky break this coincided with one of my return trips from the ditches, and I was near enough to hear the strangled snorts of the beast, the slap of the saddle leather, the uneven thud of hoofs on the hard earth, as the mare tried desperately to fling off her rider. The man's huge body seemed screwed to the saddle; his

bronze face bespoke his struggle, and short words gasped
from his half-open mouth. "Get back, over there. . . .
Head her off on the right to see if she straightens up.
. . . That's it! . . . Let her work it off."

The men tried to carry out his orders, but they couldn't
come close and so hung back, hoping for their chance.
The mare had stopped snorting. Don Segundo was silent.
A bitter clash of wills—malice and surprise the one,
control and daring the other—was going on between
them. At last the beast gave in and endured passively
the jerks of the bit that were meant to soften up her
mouth. Don Segundo made an agile leap that landed him
a safe distance from her. His vast thorax heaved, gasping
for air. His hands were cramped as if they still grasped
the hot reins; and his legs, molded by the saddle, arched
upward from the feet, as though to give solidity to his
balance and to shoulders that squared with conscious
power.

The mare was in a pitiful condition: her sweat-
drenched neck was bent with the weight of her head and
her sunken flanks trembled.

"This one ain't like the dun," said Valerio with a certain satisfaction.

"No, sir," replied the strange falsetto voice of Don
Segundo, "this one's a thoroughbred."

All of a sudden I came to: there I was sitting on my
pony with the cart hitched behind, and my mouth open
from ear to ear, under the very eye of the owner! I was
scared. In my fright I gave the poor beast a cut of the
whip and set off for the houses to the iron tune of the
pitchfork rattling and bouncing on the floor of the wagon.
Strike up the music, brother, and shake a leg!

At prayertime the owner sent for me to brew him a
couple of matés and bring them to the twilight shade of
the bead trees where he was sitting. I had to go to the
house kitchen for this, and the family cook gave me a
long song and dance as she handed me the *bombilla,*
saying the boss would take off my head if there was a
single leaf in his silver sipper. She reminded me of my
aunts. What are women for, anyway? Just for men's

pleasure. And the mean, nagging ones? For the dump heap, except that people are too soft to send them there.

The owner asked me where I was from, if I had a family, and had I been working long. I stuck pretty close to the truth, lest I fall into a trap and get sent back home.

"How old are you?"

"Fifteen." I added a year.

"That's all right."

He took his final sips. "Don't brew any more. Go to the kitchen and tell Valerio I want to see him."

There was a festive, after-supper air about the kitchen. Next day was Sunday, and the men were getting ready to go to town. The boys made pat jokes about one another, for everyone knew about the others' love affairs. Those who had families were leaving that night, to be gone until early Monday morning. The renters might decide to make the trip, too, to buy a thing or two they needed, but most of them would stay in their cabins and take it easy or get together at the big houses for a game of bowls in the clearing under the grove of mulberry trees.

The older folks complained, of course, that the fun of other days was gone: no tilting matches now, no horse races. Half asleep, I settled in a corner, close to the group made up of Don Segundo, Valerio, and Goyo, who wanted to learn how to break horses; I listened with care to the commentaries on that brutal and subtle art. Taking in the lesson, I rocked back and forth, making a sort of cradle of my stool. Bit by bit, the voices came like thoughts merged in the dying fire of the hearth. I grew conscious of one foot, because I was stepping on it with the other. The pressure of the sandal was sweet to me, and as I moved in my stool with a slow rocking motion I found the bite of the rope sole on my instep pleasurable. My aunts would have railed at me for this strange pastime; but they were far . . . so far . . . I could scarcely hear their voices mumbling a prayer, a very solemn one: why did my aunts have that voice of a priest?

Suddenly the stool on which I had fallen asleep fell over backward. My shoulders came down on a pile of wood, and the little twigs, crackling, roweled my ribs like spurs.

5

In two weeks the mares were broken. Don Segundo, patient and skilled, knew all the tricks of his art; he spent the mornings in the corral gentling his charges, getting them used to the saddle, patting them on flank, neck, and withers to wean them of their fear of hands, trimming them with great care so they would get used to the noise of the shears, and taking hold of their shoulders so they would not rear when he came close. Gradually, without roughness, he had carried out all the difficult tasks of the wrangler, and we saw him let down the bars and round up the yearlings with the freshly broken mares.

"They're gentle, now," he told the owner.

"All right," said Don Leandro. "Stay with them a few days more, and I'll have another job for you."

They were peaceful weeks for me, my only trouble being the laziness of my pony Frog. And then came the bad news. They had found out in town where I was and it might be they'd try to make me go home. But they'd have to get up early in the morning to catch this bird! I'd throw myself in the river first, or let wild dogs tear me to pieces! I was done forever with loafing around those tedious streets. Once and for all I was a free man, earning the bread I ate. I'd rather live like a mountain lion alone in the wilds than be a lapdog again under the incense-stinking skirts of those bossy, whiskered old maids! They'd never catch me with that bone! But what a pain in the neck!

I was so worried that I took no notice of what was going on around me. At last I did observe the mysterious, busy air of the men, which I couldn't account for until they told me that there was going to be a roundup, followed by a drive.

Luck was with me a second time! Hadn't I decided just a few days before to run away because Don Segundo's passing had pointed out the path to me? Well, all I'd have to do now was to follow the herd and avoid local dangers merely by shifting from one ranch to another. The question was, where would the herd go? Who would ride with it? Goyo, that afternoon, gave me the information, although it was meager.

The herd would be five hundred head; it was starting south in two days, and was bound for another ranch of Don Leandro's.

"Who rides with it?"

"Valerio goes as the head drover; Horacio, Don Segundo, Pedro Barrales, and me go as hands—unless you have different orders."

Don Segundo was even closer with his facts, and I did not yet understand the reason why those who leave show that contemptuous silence toward those who stay behind.

"Can I go?"

"If the boss says so."

"And what if he says no?"

Don Segundo looked me up and down, and his eyes stopped at the height of my ankles.

"What are you looking for?" I asked, annoyed by the fixity of his stare.

"Hobbles."

"Where are any hobbles?"

"Oh, I thought you were wearing 'em."

For a moment I didn't catch on; when I did I tried to laugh, though I knew the joke was on me.

"No, I'm not hobbled, Don. But I'm afraid the boss won't have me."

"When I was your age, I did what I felt like, without asking anybody else's permission."

I had learned my lesson. I walked away, struggling to reconcile my need to go and my fear of disappointment. Don Jeremiah seemed to be kind, so I went to him and stammered out my question. He shrugged his shoulders. "Ask Valerio. He'll tell you if he wants you."

Valerio, who was the last one from whom I could have expected consideration, said he'd talk it over with the boss and suggest that I be allowed to go at half pay. "But remember, it's no soft snap."

"I don't care."

"All right. I'll let you know tonight."

Less than half an hour later, when Valerio signaled to me from the hitching post, I put down the dishes I was washing in the kitchen and rushed out.

"Well, start getting your things together, and your ponies ready."

"You're taking me along!"

"Uh-huh."

"You talked to the boss?"

"Uh-huh."

"That's what I call a real gaucho!" I burst out, full of childish gratitude.

"We'll see what you say when the saddle has rubbed the hide off your butt."

"You bet we'll see!" was my answer.

To bluff is a good thing, because once you've made your play you've got to shut out your own honest misgivings. The die is cast, and you've got to stick with it. But if there's no audience to watch you back them up, your brave resolves are pretty sure to wilt. So now, in spite of myself, I began to wonder, once I was alone, whether I could go through with it. How *would* I talk, when the "saddle had rubbed the hide off my butt"? How would it be to sleep on the ground in the rain? Where would I find a way to hide my future tenderfoot aches? I knew none of the hardships of the rough life before me; I tried to imagine floods, to remember the talk I had heard in the saloons, to draw on the adventures and rascalities of my life as a small-town brat. It was useless. What I'd learned in my haphazard childhood was of little worth to prepare me for the life I challenged. Why the devil had they taken me from my mother and stuck me in school to learn reading, arithmetic, history, which were of no use to me now?

Well, nothing to do but stiffen your belly and stand the cinch. Moreover, my thoughts made no dent on my determination; I had learned as a kid to keep them separate from action. Forced into the dance, I'd dance, since there was no way out. And if my body gave in, my will would go on. I'd wanted to get away from the soft life, to become a man, hadn't I?

"What are you mumbling to yourself?" yelled Horacio, passing by.

"Haven't you heard?"

"What?"

"I'm going with the drive!"

"What a break for the cattle!" Horacio showed none of the admiration I expected.

"Thanks a lot. Don't you see I'll have to go on foot?"

"Oh, not too far, I hope."

"It's the truth." I was thinking of my two ponies. "Know anyone around here who'd sell me a colt?"

"Oh, you turning broncobuster?"

"I'll manage the best I can. Tell me now—know of any?"

"Sure. Not far from here, over at Cuevas' farm—might be they've got just what you need, and cheap." Having had his fun, Horacio gave me good advice.

"Thanks."

At sundown I was on my way to Cuevas' farm, which was less than a mile beyond the wood. I went on foot so the boss wouldn't see I was gone and the men wouldn't laugh at me, for they all knew I had no capital to do business with. I set out through a grove of eucalyptus, stumbling and tripping over fallen branches from too much looking back. Free of the grove, I walked easier and my sandals found a sure smooth path. I skirted a little cornfield and made for the cabin.

I was walking along, thinking how to make my offer to buy and pay later. If it seemed a good thing, I decided, I'd return next day with the cash and take the colt. Suddenly, in the corn that edged my path, I heard the crackling of stalks; instinctively I shied for cover. Amidst the green leaves emerged the face of a half-breed girl, laughing and brown, and a teasing little hand waved farewell. I blushed with rage at my silly scare and walked on.

A huge bay dog started for me; just as I was whipping out my knife, his master called him off. I was close to the buildings: a low 'dobe house profusely thatched with straw and in front a patio that much water and much sweeping had hardened like a floor. In the small corral I saw a dozen horses, among them a fawn-colored colt.

"Good afternoon, sir," I said.

"Afternoon, friend."

"I'm one of the hands at the big house. They tell me you have a colt for sale."

The man's sly eyes studied me; I could sense a smile behind the whiskers.

"You're the buyer?"

"If you've no objections."

"There's the colt over there. You can have him for twenty pesos."

"Can I take a look at him?"

"Sure. Take a good look."

After a short inspection that wasn't any too revealing, so muddled was I by the grandeur of my role, I turned to the owner. "Tomorrow, if it's agreeable to you, I'll come for him and bring you the money."

"You're not a hard fellow to do business with."

I stood awhile, not knowing what to say, and as the man seemed more inclined to silent irony than to jesting, I raised my hand to my hat and turned toward the path by which I had come. The bay dog started for me again, but his master knew how to make himself obeyed. Just the same, I was a bit scared and started running toward the cornfield, where I would feel freer of those uncomfortably searching eyes.

About twenty yards ahead of me, a slight figure appeared and began walking in the same direction. By the red bandanna on her head and the light dress I recognized the girl. I started after the lithe body, without asking myself why, keeping close to the edge of the cornfield. She heard my steps, turned, and recognizing me as I came close, burst into the laughter of shining white teeth and eyes wide in a brown face.

I've never been afraid, except of grown women, maybe, joking because what they are looking for is bigger game. But now I was filled with a strange and troubling exaltation. To get over it, I said imperiously; "What's your name?"

"My name's Aurora."

The joy of her and the cunning of her eyes did away with my fears.

"Aren't you afraid some mountain lion might get you, running around all by yourself in a cornfield?"

"No mountain lions around here."

Her smile grew more provocative. Her young breasts rose in mounds and angles.

"There might be one come from far off," I said meaningly.

"It wouldn't be a man-eater."

Here was scorn against my pride. I put out my hand; she retreated, and then I felt that for nothing in the world could I let her go. I leaped at her and held her in my arms despite her stubborn defense and threats.

"Let me go or I'll yell!"

I dragged her into the shelter of the green corn, which traced innumerable paths in all directions. Her resistance hampered me; I stumbled over a furrow, and we fell on the soft earth together. Aurora laughed, forgetful now of the body she'd been defending, and I was able to do whatever I wanted. She lay, a single moment, quiet; her face contracted, her mouth half open, as if she were in pain. Then she laughed again.

I was proud of myself.

"Do you love me, sweet?" I could not help asking.

Aurora pushed me away with an angry shove, and got to her feet.

"Idiot! Scoundrel! The nerve of you! Just because you're stronger."

I let her go, very dignified, murmuring things to herself to console her modesty and pride.

6

My own eagerness wakened me at three in the morning. Starting at daybreak with the herd! Headed for the Unknown! I reined myself in as best I could by trying to recall all the things that had to be done and telling myself that a slip now would be bitterly paid for later. My saddle outfit was in the stable of the stallions, where I had left it because it was so near the hitching post; the pony I would ride the first hours was out in the corral, with his mate and my new one, probably, alongside Goyo's string of horses. My extra clothes were in a pile at the foot of the bed. Tobacco? I had a pack of the makings and papers. Having made a mental inventory of my possessions, I was glad to find that the preparations for this first momentous journey were not so difficult. The boss had ordered an advance of twenty-five pesos to be paid me from my first month's wages; that was enough for the colt with a little left over for my "vices."

What more could I ask for? Three ponies—one of them, it's true, an unbroken colt that might have a trick or two in store for me; outfit complete with reins, bridle, hobbles, lasso, and straps; a change of clothing if I got wet, and a stout poncho against cold and damp. Many a regular herder starts off with less.

While I checked, I was strapping on my spurs, and now I rose to my feet proud but somewhat wistful as I took in the tiny room and its cot, bare and pitiful as a skinned sheep. Ranch life, farewell! It's the open road ahead and the trackless pampas!

I bundled my two changes into the poncho, tied it around my waist, and tiptoed out, stopping at the door a moment because the darkness can be treacherous and there's no sense in rushing ahead blindly. I breathed deep the breath of the sleeping fields. The darkness stretched serene; fireflies, like sparks of a roaring blaze, gladdened it. I let the silence enter me and felt the stronger for it, and larger. Far off, a bell tinkled—someone catching a horse or getting his ponies together. The steers, as yet, gave no sign of the agitation within them, but I could smell the heavy presence of their five hundred bodies.

Suddenly I heard the gallop of horses; a bell showered its quick notes into the night; and the sounds spread through the gradually dawning day like ripples on the still surface of a pool when a pebble is tossed into it. Somewhere a cock crowed, awakening the reply of the *teros*. Isolated expressions of daily living that amplified the immensity of the world.

In the corral I caught my pony, which was restless with the unaccustomed movements of its free companions. As I put the halter on him, I felt the dew on his forehead. I could hear the rasp of Goyo's spurs against the moist earth as he looked around for something.

"Morning, brother," I said softly.

"Morning."

"Lost something?"

"Uh-huh. My whip."

"Which whip?"

"The one with the silver handle."

"It's up in the room against the trunk."

"Good. I'll get it."

"No maté?"

"In a little while."

While Goyo hunted his quirt, I saddled my sleepy pony; he snorted and jerked his ears in disgust, I whistled. Then I went to the kitchen, where I found Pedro Barrales and Don Segundo with Goyo.

"Good day."

"Good morning."

Horacio came in, stretching for all he was worth.

"You're going to rupture yourself," said Goyo, laughing.

"Not a chance. Just smoothing out the wrinkles."

Valerio silently passed the threshold and squatted in a corner to put on his shining silver buck spurs. We all sat around the fire and the maté began its rounds. Every man was alive only for himself, and my gladness suddenly became inward and grave. An outsider would have thought us all downcast by some calamity.

Since I couldn't talk, I watched.

They all seemed bigger, stronger; the open road of the morning was in their eyes. They were no longer farmhands; they had become men of the pampas. For the soul of the herder is the soul of the horizon. Even their dress had changed from the day before: rougher, more practical, all suggestive of the work ahead. The raw might of these silent men mastered me; I do not know whether it was through fear or reverence, but I held my head low and kept my feelings to myself.

Outside, the horses began neighing.

Don Segundo got to his feet, went out a moment, and came back with a pair of heavy rawhide reins.

"Boy, bring me some tallow." Slowly he greased the thick leather; after three or four rubbings it lost its whiteness.

Valerio packed his few clothes in a poncho and strapped it around his waist above the belt. Pedro Barrales looked out at the night, gave the bench a sonorous whack with his quirt, and said with a grimace of resignation, "By noon, I reckon, the sun'll make our brains boil."

There was no need of anyone's giving the word: as one man we got up and went out. Spurs clicked in chorus, leaving rows of dots in the dust. The night was growing faint. At the hitching rail each of us took his horse and set out for the fields.

"Goyo," said Valerio, "get the horses moving, and we'll round up the herd. You, kid, go with Goyo. . . . It's time to get going."

It was the foreman's first order; it was a parenthesis between the life that had gone before and that which would follow.

Valerio, Horacio, and Barrales cantered to the nearby pen where the dim, massed forms of the steers could be seen lying. Goyo and I opened the corral gate and the horses soon fell into groups, each around its bell mare, whose bell was their will.

"Open the big gate," said Goyo, "and stand by so they don't pile out too fast."

My work had begun, and with it my pride was born— the pride of sharing in the most masculine of all occupations. I had to put spurs to my pony and dash from side to side to hold back the sallies of the horses eager for freedom, but soon the experienced bell mares understood what I wanted and started quietly down the road. With the mares well in hand, I could laugh at the flare-up of the friskiest follower. A whistle and a "Back, pony!" pulled them up short. I rode along serenely, knowing I was being followed.

From the field came the shouts and alarums of the moving herd; it was the rumor of war with drums, commands, complaints, races, collisions, and upsets. It was coming nearer, swelling as it came, and we could now make out the momentous mosaic of colors and shapes in the dawn. The herd grew calm as it moved, until it was a single mass of motion with me at its prow, like a figurehead. And while dawn worked on the world, my aloneness made me suddenly sad. Why should this be? Perhaps melancholy went with the job? That morning in the kitchen I had not heard laughter; the solemn faces had surprised me. Was it that they were leaving something behind—the flash of a doubt lest they never return to their fields and families? That wouldn't explain my case, for I did not know what it was to be homesick. Maybe the women and the young ones? What was that to me? A face I had forgotten in the rush of getting ready flashed suddenly before my eyes. Aurora! But what was Aurora to me, except the casual partner in what our immature sensuality made a game without passion? Just the same, the picture of her face did not fade. I wondered what she would be doing now? Maybe she was a bit sad, in spite of the smile she had given me for a good-bye the night before in the corn patch?

At the thought of tears on that gay little face, my heart grew tender.

"Chinita," I said almost aloud, and bit the handle of my whip, and stared hard ahead in order to get my mind on something else. The day was rising in the east, vibrant and potent. My pony pranced as if he were calling up the morning. And already a bird wheeled its way above the pampas. The memory of my last two hours on the ranch ripened sweet and delicate with distance.

The day after my first encounter with Aurora I had gone back across the cornfield to wind up my purchase, and on the way home she was in the same place, but with a pout on her little mouth.

"Good afternoon."

"Hello," she said.

"Are you mad?"

"Of course I am. Why wouldn't I be? Last night, just because of you, I lost my ring somewhere here in the corn, and Mamma gave me a licking."

"Want me to look for it?" I asked, none too innocently.

"You remember where it was?"

"Do I remember!"

"Silly!"

Then we looked together for the little trinket, and what we found was our pleasure.

That afternoon she was not cross with me, and when we parted, it was not I who said "I'll wait for you tomorrow."

Poor kid! That tomorrow never came. A river to ford

brought my mind back where it belonged. The milling and alarums began anew; the frightened herd swung backward and forward till the first steers plunged into the stream. Foam rose on the stiff current—and laughter and collisions. We came out on the other side with dripping cinches and more than a splash on our breeches.

Over the earth, suddenly darkened, an enormous sun rose, and I felt I was a man to whom life is good. A man with a will of his own, and everything a good gaucho needs, even a loving country girl to mourn his departure.

7

With sunrise came a fresh breeze bringing us gladness eager to turn itself into motion. We left the river behind us, cut across the corner of a meadow, and came through a barred gate to the open trail. It ran between wire fences like a brook between its banks, and the gait of the herd grew measured, the danger of a stampede more remote. I reined in my pony and drew to one side to wait for Goyo; I wanted somebody to talk to.

"You've still got time to go back" were his first words.

"Sure thing!"

Without moving, I watched the herd go past. The yearlings moved along, monotonous and dragging. A few lowed and kept looking back to the ranch. Occasionally one made a pass with his horns; a space would open around him and fill up again with the slow tireless mass. When the brutes came by me, they veered and looked at me uneasily. Some stopped puffing through their nostrils, and sniffed. Caught up in the potent moving mass of shoulders, the rhythmic sway of heads, I sat

49

waiting for the herders while the early sun slanted down on the glistening bodies, gilding their profiles and elongating their shadows gamboling on the ground in huge grotesques.

Soon I became the butt of jokes.

"They're too bunched up for you to count," said Pedro Barrales, laughing.

"No," said Horacio, "what he's doing is picking the one he wants to rope."

"Oh, boy," cried Valerio, "I can already see you buttup on your saddle trying to cool your rump off a bit!"

"You're roping me before I run," I came back at them. "Give a fellow a chance."

The conversation went on in shouts, while one here, one there, we rained thumps on the steers who straggled or wanted to turn back.

"Remember last time," began Pedro, "the trip to Las Heras—remember, Horacio? When Venero Luna went along to learn the ropes? The noise that Christian made! Showing off before the cattle. He had a voice like a bugle and all you heard, all day, was 'Git over there, cow! Git on over there, cow!' But five days of riding took the starch out of him, and when we arrived he could hardly move a muscle. 'Over, cow!' he'd say, so soft you'd think he was prayin'. And he was so skinny and worn out I felt like tying him to my saddle straps."

"It's the truth," said Valerio sententiously. "We're all good—at the start."

They paused a moment, savoring the pride of their strong bodies. What boy hasn't had a whirl at the work? Yet there were not too many men ready to see it through, to stand, without complaint, the hard marches in winter and summer, the blister of the sun, the drench of rain, the bite of frost, the subtle treacheries of fatigue. Doubt made me flinch as I repeated what Valerio had said: "We're all good—at the start." Was I going to drop out in the first lap? Well, who knows, but at least at the moment I was full of spunk and far from down. And I was sure of one thing: they'd have to kill me before I'd admit I was tired or shirk any danger of the drive. I felt so brave that I made up my mind, the first stop, to saddle my bronco and prove there was no yellow in me. With the sun still rising, how can your hopes help rising too? I was perhaps following the morning's example.

Meantime, while my self-trust grew, we had come to a country store. It was a single building, rectangular-shaped; the taproom was an open room on the right with benches where we sat side by side like swallows on a wire. The storekeeper handed out the drinks through a heavy iron grating that caged him in with tiers of brightly labeled bottles, flasks, and jugs of every kind. Skin sacks of maté leaf, demijohns of liquor, different-shaped barrels, saddles, blankets, horse pads, lassos, covered the floor. And through this welter of stock the owner had made a narrow trail as cows make a path, and he came and went along it carrying drinks, smokes, maté, saddle fittings. Across from the taproom were a couple of cement columns supporting an arbor that joined the eave of the house to the patio of gnarled bead trees. And farther off was a *taba* field. The trail in front of the store bellied out wide enough to hold the herd.

It must have been eight o'clock when we dropped from our saddles for a bite of food; it was getting hot and we were starved. We'd been on the move five hours, with nothing under our belts but a couple of matés.

Horacio and Goyo kindled the fire and started to roast our meat. The rest went up to the bar, chatted with the owner, whom they knew from earlier drives, ordered their gins and mineral waters.

"What'll you have?" Don Segundo asked me.

"A peach brandy."

"You'll scorch your throat."

"It'll be all right, Don."

Silent, we drained our glasses. Later, one by one, we took our chunk of meat, and I washed it down with another brandy.

We were refreshed and cheered and ready to start. Don Segundo and Valerio changed mounts. Valerio saddled a roan with an arched neck we all envied because of his lively air and his delicate legs and hoofs.

"What a horse for tilting at a ring," said Pedro Barrales.

"Still a little skittish," said Valerio, "and not above playing me a dirty trick when I give him a taste of the spurs."

"Some day he'll have to learn."

Valerio got on his back, flicked him with the spur, and we saw at once how right he was. The roan was up "like boiling milk." Small and agile, the man followed the mazes of the bucking to perfection: the turns, twists, drops, balances, and spirals. His poncho kept time to the lovely wrath of the brute who at every buck displayed his slender curves like the leap of a dorado. Its withers contracted, tense with power. Its head almost touched the ground, brushing from side to side, as though saying no. But high on its arched back it bore the smiling, dominant rider, whose skilled hand at last put a stop to the contest. Laughing and panting, Valerio said, "Didn't I tell you?"

"Hm," remarked Pedro. "You can't give that fellow much rein."

"If I don't keep at him, he'll surely go bad on me."

"It'd be a crime. He's one fine pony."

The battle and the two gulps of brandy had gone to my head; I remembered my plan of the morning.

"Hey, who'll help me saddle my colt?"

"What for?"

"To ride him."

"He's going to make you sweat."

"What of it?"

"I'll help you," said Horacio. "I want that cup of coffee at your wake tonight."

Full of laughter and wisecracks, they caught my pony and saddled it so quickly I didn't have time to realize what I was in for. Horacio gave the bronco's ears a couple of tugs. "Now, brother, say the word."

I came up cautiously, put a foot in a stirrup, and threw my leg across gingerly, so as not to rouse him too soon.

The jokes had made me nervous. Which way would the colt start off? How could I tell what he was going to do? But there was nothing for me now but to go ahead. I took my courage in my two hands, settled in my seat the way I judged best, and gave the order: "Let 'er go!"

The pony didn't budge. As for me, I could hardly see. I guessed more than saw the long skinny neck in front of me, absurdly twisted to one side. At the same time I noticed that my hands were sweating, and I was afraid the reins might slip. . . .

"Goin' to stand there all day?" said a voice I couldn't place. I felt a shame that was worse than a blow: to sit there waiting was ridiculous. Blindly, I brought the quirt down on the pony's neck. I felt a painful jerk in my knees and lost all sense of balance. To make matters worse I leaned forward, and the next buck gave me a jolt on the bottom that went thudding through my whole body. My eyes opened as I felt myself falling, and this time I threw myself backward, for I had seen the road rising toward me and the pony's head and neck had disappeared. Again and again he bucked, until it seemed my bones were coming loose. But I hugged tight with my knees, and encouraged by the "Give it to him!" of my companions, I gave him another cut. The bucks followed thick and fast. There must have been a hundred; my legs stiffened in a cramp; one pad came loose from the crupper and I thought it was all over. The saddle slipped from under me. I felt myself flying through space and thrust out a hand at—nothing. I came to earth so heavily on hip and shoulder that I was stunned. However, I managed to get up.

"You hurt?" asked Valerio, who had kept close to me during my whole sorry display.

"No, brother, it's nothing," I said, forgetting the respect I owed the boss.

Thirty yards off, Don Segundo had roped the flying brute and I ran toward him.

"Hold him for me!"

"You want us to have a real corpse to cry over?" said Goyo, laughing.

"No, I mean it. Just hold that son of a bitch. I'm going to bust him wide open."

"You wait till tomorrow," Valerio sternly ordered. "This is a business trip—not a circus."

"Seems to me," said Don Segundo, "if this bird don't quiet down we may have to send him back to his aunts' cage."

Horacio brought me bridled the pony the Festal boy had borrowed.

8

Impressions are swift on the pampas, disjointed, vanishing with our tracks into the enormous present. So it was that all faces again became impassive and I speedily forgot my failure, without aftertaste. The trail was the same trail; the sky remained blue; the air, though a little hotter, smelled as sweet and the gait of my fresh pony was only the least bit livelier. The herd moved along well. The leaders trotted ahead, their bells sounding clear and steady. The daybreak lowing had ceased. But the clatter of hoofs seemed to increase and the dust grew white and thicker.

Animals and men were possessed by one fixed idea: continual movement.

At times a young steer lagged to nibble a mouthful of grass by the way and had to be urged on.

The swaying mass caught me in its rhythm and I moved along dozing with open eyes. It seemed that one might keep on like this forever, without thought, without strain, lulled in the cradle of the horse's stride, and with the nip of the sun on back and shoulder as the needed hint to carry on. By ten o'clock the skin on my back seemed to be steaming. My pony's neck was drenched with sweat and the ground rang more hollow under the quick hoofs. By eleven my hands and veins were swollen. My feet had gone to sleep. My bruised hip and shoulder ached. The steers moved more cumbrously. The pulse in my temples throbbed dizzily. The pony's shadow shrank so slowly that it was maddening. By twelve we rode on our own shadows, and this made the sun's power over us more ruthless. No air stirred; the dust rose in a yellowish cloud as if to hide us. Long threads of slobber trickled from the mouths of the yearlings. The horses dripped sweat, and salty gobs ran from their foreheads into their eyes. I wanted sleep, sleep and nothing else.

We came at last to the ranch of a certain Don Feliciano Ochoa. The shade of the grove was a delight of coolness. Valerio got permission for us to turn the herd into a grassy corral where there was water. When we dropped from the saddle, our clothes were stuck to our flesh and we waddled like new-hatched ducklings. Our spurs tripped us as we shambled toward the kitchen. We said hello to the ranch hands, took off our hats to cool our sweaty heads, and drank the matés they gave us. Then we livened up the fire and spitted our beef on the hearth. I took no part in the talk that soon sprang up between the home outfit and us strangers. My body felt like a cut of dried beef, and all I could think of was to eat and then stretch out even if it was only on the brick floor.

"Going on, after you've eaten?"

"No, sir," said Valerio. "The weather's too sultry for the herd. We were thinking, if you don't mind, that we'd stay here for a siesta and travel some at night, God willing."

I could have jumped for joy. I immediately felt my limbs stretch soothingly into rest and my good humor returned like magic. "Great!" I cried and spat without lifting my head. One of the ranch hands looked at me and smiled.

"You're new at this?"

"Sure," I murmured as if to myself. "But the shine's rubbing off."

"Oh," said the old man. "You've got a long pull ahead of you yet."

"He's a fast worker, though," said Pedro Barrales. "He had a whirl at a bronco today. And he kept on with his quirt, even when he was flying over the brute's head. He's one of them that dies fighting."

"Good lad!" The old man's eyes were warm. "Here's a sweet maté for a good gaucho."

"I'll deserve it, Don, when the animal can't throw me."

"That'll be tomorrow."

"At that," Goyo spoke up, "I don't know but what it might be better to turn the beast loose."

"Sure," said I. "And see my twenty pesos take it on the run."

"You said it," the old man broke in again, "the lad doesn't have to look in his pocket for answers."

"Oh," said Don Segundo, "no worry about his tongue. His mouth would have to swell shut before he'd stop talking. He belongs to the parrot family."

"Here's where I take a licking." I hunched my shoulders as if for a blow and kept quiet.

A kid of about twelve came over and sat beside me. He looked at my spurs, my blistering hands, my face still dusty from the drive, with the same wonder I had shown days back for Valerio and Don Segundo. His ingenuous display of admiring curiosity stamped me as a real cowboy. Then he took it upon himself to show me a good place where I could take my siesta, and I was as thankful for this as for his silent homage.

At four in the afternoon we were again on the trail. The farewells had been cordial; a few matés, a wash-up, and a thorough dusting of my shirt made me a new man. I could hear the water sloshing in my pony's belly; the herd had had time to lie down and have some mouthfuls of grass and was in better spirits. Besides, before us lay the promise of the cool night, and hope lives when things are visibly getting better and a real rest is ahead. As when we left the ranch, I rode in front of the herd, where I could watch the road and the far villages, storing up forever in my mind the first treasures of the apprentice herder. Two hours later, as we were passing a farmhouse, Goyo came up with an order from Valerio.

"Follow me. We're going to butcher a sheep and then catch up with the herd."

"I'm no good at that kind of work, brother."

"No? Then here's where you learn."

The herd moved on, and we dismounted at the house.

"A sheep?" said the owner, greeting us like old friends. "Right away." Nothing was said about price.

Goyo was quick and clever; my own fussy uselessness kept him laughing. I had no more than slit the skin of one foot when his knife tip, traveling across the paunch, had reached mine. His long strokes separated the hide from the flesh, and when he'd made a slit as big as his hand, he skinned the beast like a glove. Circling the joints with his knife, he broke the four feet. Between tendon and shinbone, he made a slit, fastened the buckle of his bridle in it, threw the free end over the branch of a tree, and we both pulled till the animal swung in the air. Now, quickly, he opened the belly, pulled out fat and guts in slippery layers, scoured away the entrails and lungs, heart and liver from the thorax.

"And what did you want *me* for?" I asked, standing stupidly beside him, ashamed of my own hands, which hung there as useless as refuse.

"You're going to help me carry the meat."

When the animal was dressed, we halved it, put it into two burlap bags which we hung to our saddles, and said good-bye to the owner. He sent a skinny, sullen, half-breed girl to us with a couple of matés, and then we set off at a jog trot for the not-too-distant herd.

My ignorance about butchering troubled me more than getting thrown that morning, and I rode a bit ahead of Goyo, boiling with rage. When the kid at Don

Feliciano's was admiring my gear, I'd seen only the bright side of my job; I didn't remember that the bitter goes with the sweet; I only recalled it when my tenderfoot ignorance came up against the realities. How many more disillusions, I wondered, were lying in wait! Before I went around putting on airs, I'd better learn to butcher, to rope both riding and standing, to make bridles, reins, and hobbles, to shear a sheep, to clip a horse, to throw the *bolas,* to trim hoofs, to cure distemper, spavin, and heaven knows what else! The thought of it all took my breath and heart away. And I muttered to myself, "It's one thing to sing alone and another to sing to the guitar."

While I wrestled thus with myself, we had overtaken the herd, but I went on ahead and alone. Now the afternoon surprised me by fading away. I was suddenly scared by my own solitude and turned back to find out when we would eat.

It was to be a supper in the open. We stopped in a grove of willows by the trail, gathered dry branches, and made a fire. The ruddy flame turned our faces to copper as we squatted in a circle, and our hands, busy with meat and knife, showed hard and gleaming. All was peace except for the tinkle of cowbells and the homesick lowing of the herd. Frogs croaked in the canebrake, punctuating the monotonous chirp of crickets. At lazy intervals the *chajás* denounced our presence. The green twigs hissed in the blaze and exploded like faroff firecrackers. The ache of utter fatigue moved from one part of my body to another, and my head felt as though it was smothered beneath a saddle pad.

We had no water and would have to endure thirst for hours more.

Again, at the herd's pace, we took to the road. Above us the starred heaven was a single immense eye full of the shining sands of sleep. But each step drove a herd of agonies through every muscle in my body. How much more of this would I have to bear?

By now I couldn't tell whether the herd was one animal trying to be many or many animals wanting to be one. The disjointed movement of the huge whole made me

sick to my stomach, and if I looked down when my
pony veered or turned its head, the earth seemed to
heave like a shapeless fleshy mass. If only I could go to
sleep in my saddle like the veterans! Nobody paid the
least attention to me. They were all watching the animals to make sure none strayed. From time to time
someone let out a whoop. The *teros* screeched as we
passed and the little owls began to play hide-and-seek,
calling to one another from velvety throats.

Not a town in sight!

All of a sudden I realized we'd arrived! Close by was
the broad dark outline of buildings, and the trail wid-
ened like a river flowing into a lake.

Goyo, Don Segundo, and Valerio, I heard, were going
to stand watch. We were in the fairgrounds outside a
village.

Near the other horses I unbridled my pony and
slipped off his saddle. I threw the outfit on the ground
under a zinc shed and dropped on it the way a chunk
of mud falls off a cartwheel.

A whiplash, which I hardly felt, fell across my shoulder blades.

"Toughen up, boy."

It seemed to me it was the voice of Don Segundo.

9

Goyo had to take me by the feet and drag me three yards to wake me.

"God, what a sleepyhead! I was about to try the way we get an armadillo out of its hole."

"Time to go?"

"Pretty soon."

I tried to get up, but I couldn't.

"What's the matter? Can't stand up?"

"On all fours," I answered while I somehow managed to get to my feet.

"Where's it hurt?" Goyo laughed.

"Where I fell," I lied, not wanting to admit how exhausted I was.

"Here?"

"Ouch!" I yelled and jerked loose the arm he was squeezing. But that was a farce. Where it hurt, really, was in my stomach, my groin, my thighs, my calves, and my shoulders.

"Maybe you've got a chill?"

61

"It'll go, soon as I move around."

Laboriously I managed to walk without showing how it hurt. An overcast day was reluctantly breaking.

"Going to rain?"

"Yes."

"Where's Don Segundo?"

"With the horses, saddling up."

Guided by the tinkling of the bells, I kept on till I could see the man's huge silhouette magnified by the darkness.

"Good morning, Don Segundo."

"Good morning, boy. I want to talk to you."

"What is it, Don?"

"You going to saddle up that bronco of yours again?"

"Why not?"

"Good! Then I'll help you so you don't make a spectacle of yourself. No one'll see us here. You do exactly what I tell you."

I saw him draw his rope from the saddle. Then he took my bridle, examined the halter—a stout one—and told me to come along. Through the dull light of the threatening dawn he went toward my brown pony, unrolling his lasso. The drowsy bronco didn't have a chance. The loop caught him high on the neck, and Don Segundo held him without even troubling to steady the rope against his thigh.

"Go get your saddle."

When I returned, the horse was tied to a post, haltered and bridled. Patiently Don Segundo placed, one by one, the sheepskin pad, the cross straps, the cinch on its back. When he tightened the strap the colt started to make a fuss, but it was too late; cushions soon made the saddle ready. I watched the man with amazement; he was treating my bronco like a stray lamb.

All the time he was fastening the cinch, untying the pony, and leading him over to the open field, Don Segundo was giving me instructions.

"You mustn't be foolish," he said. "Lot of those riders you see started green and had to use their wits to learn. Once you're up, you grab hard and hold on tight—I'm not going to tell on you. And don't let go till you feel good and safe. Understand?"

"Uh-huh."

"Let's go, then."

His horse was two paces from me, ready to come to my rescue. But before I mounted, I looked around; despite what I'd been told by the man I respected more than anyone else in the world, I didn't want anyone else to catch me cheating. There was no one, and cautiously I got up, my legs trembling. The pain in my thighs and groin was so bad I could hardly bear it. But this was no time to give in, and I stood it as best I could.

"Hold him now till I mount."

The pony, as if he understood, kept still until my teacher was at my side.

Don Segundo raised his whip. The pony lifted his head and started off without trying any tricks. We made a long run around the field. Little by little I began to feel surer of myself and challenged my pony by giving him a taste of the spur. He answered with a few long bucks, but I weathered them without needing to follow Don Segundo's advice.

"He's broke already!" I said.

"Don't be too sure," Don Segundo answered simply. No detail of my behavior had escaped him. Riding first on one side, then on the other, he guided my pony to the turn of the road where the others were having their matés. They greeted us with a shout.

All puffed up with pride like a turkey gobbler I finished off the job by reining in my pony according to my master's orders.

"Now to the left. Now to the right. Now, steady, till he backs."

With every jerk of the rein I was getting stronger, until I made my victim's muzzle tremble as I had seen the others do.

"Good enough! Now get off. Take hold of the bridle and make a long jump so you'll land clear."

Aglow with confidence, I obeyed.

"Cool kid," said Pedro Barrales.

Not until I went to unsaddle did I realize that with the jerks I had rubbed the skin off my hands and my left palm was bleeding badly.

"You're hurt," said Horacio. "Leave him there and I'll unsaddle."

He didn't have to repeat his offer; sharp twinges were running up my elbow. I wrapped a handkerchief around the wound, and Pedro helped me tie it.

"The reins were stiff," I said.

"Never mind about that," Goyo intervened. "Have a sip of rum. You've earned it." I accepted with joy; that invitation to a drink seemed the best of rewards.

Half an hour later the praise and the backslappings and the drinks were over; once more we were the impassive herders. But I carried within me a wealth of satisfaction, of which I took great swallows from time to time along with the air of the young morning. Heavy clouds, piled against the horizon, had been moving in till they overspread the heavens, and as the herd swung into the narrow trail the first drops of rain came, sudden and opaque. It was early but already hot, and the cool patter was a joy to hear. Some of the men got out their ponchos; I waited.

The look of the sky told us that the rain was merely the prelude to something more serious. The earth gave off rank scents. The grass and the thistles were waiting, passionately sure; the whole countryside listened. Suddenly a fresh crackle of drops on the trail raised a fine dust cloud. The path seemed illumined as with a misty splendor. Now I put on my poncho. The rain hurled down, blotting out the horizon, the fields, even things nearby. The cowboys spread out along the herd to hem them in more closely.

"Water!" shouted Valerio as he wove in and out among the cattle. I entertained myself by feeling the steady thud of the raindrops on my body and wondered how long my poncho would protect me. My hat echoed hollowly to the blows, and rivulets began to run from it. To keep them from running down my neck I turned the brim up in front and down behind, and channeled the water onto my back. One's first response to rain, as my experience later taught me, is to laugh, although many a time no good comes of a soaking. Laughing, then, I met the first assault. But soon I had to stop thinking of myself; the herd, bewildered and blinded by the downpour, tried to wheel about and balked at going ahead.

I had to cut in among them, like the others, shoving and hitting. Every time I shouted, my mouth got full of water, which kept me constantly spitting. I realized now that my poncho was too short. In half an hour my knees were soaked, and my boots were water jars. I began to feel cold, though I could still put up a good fight against it. The kerchief around my neck no longer served me as a sponge, and down both chest and spine I felt two streams of cold.

Soon I was soaked. The wind we were breasting rose, making the punishment worse, and though it finally cleared the air a little, relief was not so quick that I did not long for it to be a lot quicker. In my distress I looked at the others, hoping for an echo of my troubles. Were they suffering too? If they were, you couldn't notice it. The water ran off their indifferent faces as off fence rails; they seemed no more affected than the fields.

The trail, which had been so bright a note in contrast to the meadows, was now a swath of gloom. Ahead of the herd it glowed like steel; behind, it was churned by the two thousand hoofs that sloshed through it with the sound of some primeval beast chewing its cud. My pony's feet kept slipping, and that made his gait easier. Here and there the hard earth seemed varnished; it mirrored the sky like a brook.

There were two hours of this. I gazed at the burnished, hostile countryside. My clothes were plastered to my body and caused a burning, like a fever at its peak, on my chest, my stomach, my thighs. I shivered continuously, my muscles twitched violently, and I said to myself that if I were a woman I would be crying my eyes out. Suddenly there came a clearing in the sky! The rain powdered into a subtle mist, and as though in answer to my great need a ray of sun fell upon the field, tripped along the rises, lost itself in the gullies, stood tiptoe on the hills. It was a promise of good things, which, hesitant for a moment, became a shower of sunshine rioting upon us.

The fence posts, the wires, the thistles, wept for joy. The sky grew enormous and light poured heavily upon the plain.

The yearlings seemed to have put on new clothes, and the horses. And we ourselves had lost the wrinkles of fatigue and heat, our skins showing taut and shining.

Our clothes steamed in the sun. I took off my poncho, opened my shirt and undershirt, and pushed my hat back on my head.

The herd smelled the freshened fields and were harder to manage. We had to keep running about, slipping, risking our limbs.

A potent life throbbed in all things. I felt new, reborn, able to withstand the meanest trick that fate might play on me. But all this vital excess remained sealed within our bodies. We would have need of it, soon enough, to help us over the tough times ahead. We did not squander ourselves in needless antics. We fell again into our sober and steadfast rhythm: Ride, ride, ride. . . .

10

I slipped the bit he had just got used to champing, loosed the hobbles as much as possible, so he might drink with comfort. The bay went down to the water, muzzled it cautiously, and then began to drink in avid swallows, without taking his quick eye off me. He was a good little chap, though a bit wild still and tricky. I watched him with the pride of owner and trainer; I was sure that some day he'd be a prize winner. The water pulsed in regular beats down his throat. He raised his head, wiped his mouth by running a long pink tongue over his muzzle. Suddenly he stood alert, his ears pricked forward, waiting for some far-off noise to be repeated.

"Weasel," I whispered softly, calling him by his name.

The bay turned, snorted at me nervously, and began to nibble the tender grass on the bank. As he grew easier, he ate gluttonously, bunching whole mouthfuls with his flexible lips and making the little stems crackle as he jerked them. My gaze fell on the river. Its barely perceptible current made a tiny eddy near where I stood, like a dimple of laughter on the cheek of a child.

This brought back a memory that had seemed lost in the dull fog of childhood. A long time before, five years if I remembered aright, I had reviewed the flavorless days of my town life and sworn to break away. It had been on the outskirts of the town, beside a brook. Not far off was a bridge, and in the middle of the brook a pool where I went swimming.

What different pictures my new life called forth! And to prove it I had only to look at my gaucho outfit, my pony, my saddle.

Blessed be the moment that lad made up his mind to flee the mean house of his aunts! But whose was the credit? I thought of Don Segundo, who had carried me along on his way through town, as he might have carried a burr growing by the road that stuck to his *chiripá*.

Five years and we had not been away from each other for a single day of our hard life! Five years, which can make a gaucho of a lad if he has the luck to spend them with a man like the one I called godfather. It was he who had guided me with care toward all the wisdom of the pampas. He had taught me the knowledge of the herder, the cunning of the wrangler; he showed me how to use the lasso and the bolas, the difficult art of training a horse to cut in on a stampeding herd and stop it, how to teach a string of ponies to stop at a word on the open pampas so that you could catch them whenever and wherever you wanted. Watching him, I had learned the ways of thongs and straps, learned to make my own bridles, reins, cinches, saddle pads, how to twist lassos, how to insert the rings and the buckles.

Under him, I became physician to my ponies: I cured sore hoof by poulticing it with mud, distemper, the way you did with a dog or by means of a halter pieced from cornhusks, weak kidneys with a plaster of rank mud over the kidney, lameness by tying a hair from the tail on the sound leg, hoof growths with a hot whetstone, boils and other ills in ways too numerous to mention.

And he taught me how to live: courage and fairness

in the fight, accepting one's fate whatever it might be, moral strength in matters of the heart, caution with women and liquor, reserve among strangers, fidelity to friends.

I even learned from him how to have a good time: from him, and none other, how to strum the guitar and how to dance. From the store of his memory I took songs to sing alone or with a partner, and by watching him learned to manage the intricate steps of the *gato,* the *triunfo,* and other gaucho dances. He overflowed with verses and stories, enough to make a hundred country lasses blush with joy or with shame.

Yet all this was nothing but a pale reflection of the fire of the man, and my wonder at him grew every day. He'd been everywhere! In every ranch he had friends who admired him, loved him, though he was always on the move. His authority with the country folk was such that a single word of his untangled the knottiest problem. But he did not exploit his popularity; it seemed rather to bore him. "I can't stay long on any ranch," he said, "because first thing you know I'm wanting to be more boss than the owner." What a *caudillo* he would have made! But above everything Don Segundo loved his freedom. His was the lone, anarchic spirit that wilts in prolonged intercourse with men. The action he loved best was continual motion; the talk he loved best, the soliloquy.

In pursuit of our work, we covered a great part of the province. Ranchos, Matanzas, Pergamino, Rojas, Baradero, Lobos, El Azul, Las Flores, Chascomús, Dolores, El Tuyú, Tapalqué, and many others had seen us plastered with mud or dust, riding tail on a herd. We knew all the big ranches: Roca, Anchorena, Paz, Ocampo, Urquiza; we knew the pampas of La Barrancosa, Las Víboras, El Flamenco, El Tordillo, where we spent the slack season between jobs.

One virtue of my godfather flowered best in the easy talk around the evening fire. He was a great teller of stories, and this gift added luster to his fame. I think his tales changed my life. By day I was always the tough,

sturdy pampas boy, fearless in the dangers of my work,
but my nights became peopled with eerie shapes; a will-o'-
the-wisp, a shadow, a cry, was enough to fill my mind
with scenes of magic, black or white. My imagination
began to take on strength and this added joy to the vast
meditations engendered by the pampas.

I'd got this far in my drowsy meditations when Weasel
shied so sharply that he almost jerked the halter from
my hand. I followed his eyes and saw the face of a fox
mocking us from across the river. I was a bit ashamed of
my daydreams, as if the sharp little beast had been laughing at me. I got up, coughed, saddled and bridled, and
started back to the ranch. Rising from the ravine, I saw
the great pasturage and far off the ranch groves. The
place was large and well stocked. It took in ten leagues,
eight tenant farms, generous orchards, well-kept sheds
and roads, a luxurious mansion and a flower garden like
nothing I had ever seen. We had been cutting out steers
and on this particular day, which was Christmas, the
squire was giving a big dance for all the hands, the
tenants, and the neighborhood.

I'd spent the morning helping to clean and trim the
shearing shed, until it was decorated like a church; and
as I rode back (for it was sundown) I promised myself
a night like I'd not had for a long time. At one of the
farms down by the canebrakes of the valley I had met a
girl, gay as a linnet. It wouldn't be a bad plan to put a
little wood on that fire.

Meantime, my bay picked his trail cautiously through
the sedge and the tall grass. Behind me lay the lagoon,
covered by a haze of tiny cries, confused and timid. I
took the wood road. The trees trembled with the dying
day.

Suddenly I came upon another rider, and my eyes hesi-
tated a moment on his face. "Aren't you Pedro?"

"Last name Barrales. That's me. I heard you were
around these parts and thought I'd look you up and find
how life was treating you."

"I might 'a' known it was you. Second I laid eyes on
those pockmarks, I says to myself: 'I know that mug!' "

"And me, brother. Why, I've missed you so much I haven't had a good piss since you left."

It was good to see the good comrade of my first drive! The memory of his gay chatter had kept tinkling in me like a bell. We rode along together to the hitching post, and he made me tell him everything I had done since we last met, while his witty comments wove a garland around my words. We arranged to go together to the dance; meantime, we ate elbow to elbow, squatting with thirty men around the spit.

Already from the hearth we could see the early carriages and riders, forerunners of the festivity, draw in to the shed. We heard the laughing women, and little by little the kitchen filled up with country folk greeting us, some shy, some sly. At last the place grew too crowded for us, and Pedro and I went out to explore the dance hall. We put up our best front, but the shed scared us: where once were bags, hides, farm machines, it was now aglow with lamps, candles, paper lanterns, flags, ready to celebrate the happiness of a hundred couples. The center of the floor, cleared and swept clean, both frightened us and drew us like a whirlpool. Chairs bordered the walls and on them sat women, many with children in their arms, staring with big frightened eyes or serenely sleeping through all the chatter, the lights, and the colors.

The older women wore dark dresses, the young ones light, flowered skirts. Some wore a scarf at their neck; others, on their head. But they all seemed rapt in mystic meditation, as if there to witness a miracle or a funeral.

Pedro gave me a sly thump on the thigh, "Patience, buddy, here comes the corpse."

We strolled from the dance shed to the tent improvised from canvas haystack covers, and here were tempting rows of bottles, mysterious hampers covered with gay cloths that hid—we guessed—cakes, meat pies, crullers. A lad sat among all these dainties, bored and half asleep.

"Pass us a bottle, buddy," said Pedro. "They're so full they might run over and we are empty."

"Sure it's not you who are full?"

"Only of wind, maybe."

"And ideas."

"Can't get tight on that, boy."

"Well, the boss doesn't want anyone tight."

"How about some cakes then?"

"Ladies first."

"Damn it," Pedro came back at him, "you're one of them hogs that's got no bacon."

The watchdog of the refreshments and the drinks gave us a grin; we went off to slick up a bit, for the guitars and accordions were tuning up and we didn't want to miss the first dance.

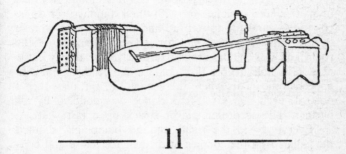

11

In the path of light thrusting from the door into the night, the men stood thick as maggots in a cheese. Pedro pushed me ahead of him and we went in, but my poor herder's clothes made me self-conscious and we stayed near the door. The girls, wrapped in their modesty, were tempting as ripe fruit, waiting in their bright attire for someone to pick them and enjoy them. I ran over the assortment; not one held me. All of a sudden I spied my girl. She wore a red dress with a sky-blue kerchief around her neck, and it seemed to me that all her coquettishness was for me alone. An accordion and a couple of guitars struck up the polka. Nobody moved.

I had the illusion that these country people were alive only in their hands. And they were heavy lumps in the laps of the women, dead weights hanging from the arms of the men; idle, they were meaningless. Suddenly all faces turned toward the door, like a field of wheat swaying in the wind. The squire, a brawny fellow, with salt

73

and pepper whiskers, greeted us with a mischievous laugh. "Now, boys, start dancing and having the good time God means you to. Come along, Remigos, and you, Pancho, and you, Don Primitivio, sir, and the rest of you. Felisario, Sofanor, Ramón, Telmo, let's get our partners."

For a moment we were pushed this way and that, and had to make way for those the squire had called on. The sound of his brisk voice had united the rest of us, as though for a cavalry charge. And in truth, it's no mean feat for men who live most of the time miles from all human contact—alone, or with their families, or some comrade—suddenly to step up and take a strange woman by the waist! A crowd had formed in the middle of the room and was milling around restlessly, like thirsty cattle at a water hole, before they could make up their minds to approach the chairs where the women sat. But once they'd done it, each man's self-importance was doubled by his partner. The accordion player struck up a fast waltz.

"Everybody to the right, and no bumping!" shouted the caller. And the couples, with their feet close and bodies drawn back to keep from touching, began to whirl around, defying dizziness and fatigue. The dance was on. After the waltz came a mazurka. Young men, old men, boys, danced solemnly, and no face betrayed the slightest pleasure. Their enjoyment was mingled with astonishment; to be touching the body of a woman, to feel beneath the hand the archaic stiffness of a corset or the soft, pliant flesh, to be joined in motion with a blushing girl, was nothing to laugh about. Only the more thoughtless gave vent to the outburst that accompanies every human emotion.

I was getting nervous at Pedro's side and feeling as out of place as if in church. Shyness and the desire to dance with my red-dressed girl were at war in me. The monotonous accordion stopped for a moment. The caller clapped his hands. "Now the chair polka!"

One of the bystanders lugged a chair awkwardly to the middle of the floor. The squire opened the dance with a girl in green who after two giddy whirls around the room was seated on the chair; she sat there all puffed up as though sitting for her portrait.

"There's a parrot for my cage!" said Pedro. But I, like everybody else, was waiting to see what would come next.

"Feliciano Gómez!"

A big country bumpkin tried to run away, but they shoved him back to the center, where he stood like a bewildered sheep.

"Let him get a look at the bait!" shouted Pedro.

The poor chap did what he could to play up to the fun but his face was full of the confusion of the simple man who suddenly finds himself conspicuous. At last he plucked up courage and took six long strides to the girl in green. She looked him over insolently from head to foot and then turned her chair around, her back to him.

The man turned helplessly to the squire. "You shouldn't try to hitch a rough nag like me, sir, to a neat little filly like that."

"Don Fabián Luna!"

An old man with a long beard and bowed legs came boldly forward and got the same treatment.

"One's too ugly," he said, "and the other's too old." And he let out a guffaw that would have scared all the ducks off a lagoon.

The squire pretended to be discouraged.

"What you want," Don Fabián advised him, "is a smarter, younger chap."

"That's it. You pick him."

"Mebbe that young herder . . ."

That was all I could hear, and it made me feel like a pony with a tight hobble, but I was up against the wall, too far from the door; there was no chance of slipping out in the night to lose myself, as I would have wished. Everyone was looking at me, and that brought back the old days when I had been the town smart aleck. So I stepped squarely over to the girl, pushed back my hat, folded my arms, and waited. The girl tried to outstare me as she had done the others.

"The longer you look at me," said I, "the surer you are to buy me."

The next moment we were whirling our two regulation turns around the room, within the circle of stares.

"I wonder what boys from the North like," said the girl as if talking to herself, when she left me in the chair.

"We tilt our hats to the right," I hinted.

She took three steps to the right, and then stopped, uncertain.

"We get off our ponies on the side of the lasso."

But seeing that my hints did not give her the needed clue, I recited this verse:

> "My girl is whiter than wheys and curd
> But she blushes red when I tell her my love."

This time she understood, and my boldness was rewarded when I led out the little brunette, though I don't know whether in step to the music or not.

At midnight they brought in trays of refreshments for the womenfolk. Wines and punch were served; cakes, pies, cookies, were passed around in willow baskets. And the ones who wanted roast meat went out to the tent. The men made a crowd around the booths where Pedro and I had looked longingly and vainly at the bottles earlier in the evening, and drank their gin, anisette, peach and cherry brandies. From that time on there was a stream of goings and comings between the dance floor and the tent, and the gaiety mounted. The accordion player was replaced by a livelier one; polkas, mazurkas leaped from his fingers with cadenzas, arpeggios and trills. Jokes grew louder; the girls laughed heartily, their careful dignity forgotten.

I danced four dances with my girl in red and to the lilt of the guitar poured out flowery compliments that she accepted with pleased blushes. Betweentimes I went back to Pedro Barrales, who entertained me with his comments.

"You're a boob," I said. "Why don't you dance? You're as glum as a shoat that's been taken from the teat."

"You think I'm as crazy as you to go jumping all over the floor?"

"Crazy?"

"So crazy the water's boiling in your head."

And as I made believe I was offended, he took me affectionately by the arm. "Don't get mad, fellow. You're like the Cruz gully: got your good side and your bad."

"Then here's to the good one!" And I went back to my fandango.

The excitement kept rising and we danced faster and faster rhythms, when the caller again clapped his hands, "Now then, folks, let's have a *gato* sung like it should be and danced by them that know the steps!"

The accordion player made room for the guitarist who was going to sing. Two couples took their place near the musicians. The women kept their eyes on the ground and the men turned up their hat brims. The guitars began to strum. Flexible wrists swayed above the strings with rhythmic motion; sharp twangs marked the accent, cutting short the murmur of the bass strings like a knife. The intermittent lash of the measure began to irradiate daring in the air like a drum roll. The dancers stood waiting for the vibrant fires of the music to become the very soul of their long-fibered muscles, of their lithe, slow backs, of their eager shoulders.

Gradually the room became drenched in the music. The white walls enclosing the tumult were as though steeped in the song.

The door cut four rigid lines into an endless and starry night above fields that cared only for sleep. The candles trembled like old grandmothers. The floor tiles were ready to echo under the feet of the dancers. Everything had succumbed to the proud male strum of the music.

The singer expressed his tenderness in tense tones:

"All I need is a ladder of love.
 All I need is a ladder of love
 To reach the heaven of your throat, my life."

The two women and the two men began the dance.
The men moved agile and insistent, like amorous cocks
pursuing a hen. The women stepped ahead inside the de-
scribed circle and sent coquettish glances over their
shoulders. The group made a turn, and the singer continued:

"Fly, unhappy one, fly, I'm going to sea
 In a little boat, my life, in a little boat."

The women picked up their skirts with careful fingers
and opened them fanwise, as if to receive a gift or de-
fend something. Shadows flickered on the walls, touched
the roof, and fell like rags to be trod on by gallant steps.
A sudden haste roused the two male bodies. Their colt-
skin boots rustled and shuffled a prelude; heels and soles
clicked a multiplying rhythm that caught the guitars' ac-

cent to mark it and make it happy. The moving folds of the *chiripás* sounded like faint waters. But the dance steps grew vigorous as a bronco's leaps, complementing in resonant counterpoint the melody of the strings.

Turn and heel-tapping were repeated. A guitar strummed four measures alone. Then the dance fell back into long steps. But the heels and spurs sounded again in muted agitation. The skirts spread more sumptuously than ever; the percale gleamed like little fields of clover blossoming in rustic splendor.

The dance died on a hard, emphatic note.

Several of the women pursed their lips in disdain at these country dances, trying to ignore them. But an involuntary gladness took possession of us all, for we felt that here was the pantomime of our loves and delights.

I took part in one dance with Don Segundo and my girl.

It was a *gato* with words. When silence had made a ring around us, I spoke out my verses clearly:

> "To come to this dance a star was my guide,
> For I knew that here was the one I liked."

We gave a turn to the right and tapped out a figure. I waited quietly for the answer that came without delay:

> "I know nothing of this love you're talking about
> But if you teach it well, I'll soon find out."

Next was Don Segundo's turn, and he advanced, challenging his partner:

> "One, two, three, four,
> If you don't love me, everything's o'er."

Doña Encarnación, his stout partner, made her turn and with an indifferent shrug of her broad shoulders replied:

"One, two, three,
    A lot it matters to me!"

The verse play went on, alternating jest and gallantry.

We danced a *triunfo* and *prado;* my little brunette and I got so warmed up that we sent signals to each other that, as they were in verse, seemed to us hidden from the crowd.

One of the girls sang. A man had to improvise an answer in rhymed couplets, for that's the custom. But who would dare pace the room from one end to another, declaiming original, versed jokes amid the silence of the rest? Don Segundo was suddenly in the middle of the ring.

All were hushed with excitement. My godfather took off his hat and passed his forearm over his brow, a sign of hard thinking. At last he seemed to find his inspiration. He gave a glance around the room, and his strong voice broke out:

"I'm an old ram from the San Blas flock."

He turned slowly on his heels:

"You've seen me from the front."

He moved, slow and indifferent, toward the door, and as he disappeared, added in a bored tone:

"Now have a look at my back."

My brunette was the liveliest little morsel at the party, and as the coming dawn suggested the idea of pleasant rest, I let myself drown in her sparkling eyes and in the laughter of her full mouth made for amorous answers. Stirred by my own compliments and her acceptance of them, I tried to get her alone by inviting her to go to the tent for refreshments. It took a lot of careful maneuvering, but at last I got her out of sight behind the improvised restaurant. I took her hand and without further ado tried to kiss her. We struggled a moment and she repulsed me with a look of anger. Not knowing how to make amends, I took her back to the dance. Three times I asked her for a dance and she turned me down each time with a trivial excuse.

By now I was mad, and I remembered the girl in green. In no time I was on the best terms with her, and I began calling myself a fool for all the time I had wasted on the other. Tenderly, as we finished a polka I squeezed her hand. But I was out of luck that night! For she squared off in front of me and asked scornfully, "You think I'm a broom to sweep up other people's leavings?"

That was good-bye to my fun for the night. The crowd shoving up against me got on my nerves like a horse that had given one a hard time at a roundup.

I took refuge in Pedro's company.

"Look!" He pointed at a couple of gringos who were bobbing along as they danced. "Aren't they the grand

gauchos, the way they're pulling out nails with their heels?" Then he saw my glumness and turned his jokes on me. "Didn't I tell you no good comes of hopping around like a monkey on a stick? Did they do you dirt, pal? Poor kid! You look like someone's taken away your bottle."

I fled into the breaking day to spread my saddle blanket and get a few hours' sleep.

12

It was our last night. We sat in a circle with a round of matés, having eaten and exhausted the stock of questions and answers about the route we were to take next day. Brief words fell like ashes of thought. We were absorbed in slight worries, about horses or saddle outfits, and it was as if the horizon that stretched before us on the morrow had settled on us now in the silence. I recalled my first drive.

Perico, who hated doing nothing, said we were as droopy as hens before a storm. "Let's either turn in," he said, "or have Don Segundo tell us one of those tales of witches and magic, more mixed-up than a peddler's pack."

"Since when do I know stories?" demanded Don Segundo.

"Bah! Don't make yourself out dumber than you are. Tell us the one about the fox and the Englishman and the ranch widow."

"You must have heard that one from someone else."

"From your lying mouth we heard it. But if you don't want to tell that one, how about the colored girl Anicota who married the devil to have a look at his tail?"

Don Segundo settled back on his stool, as if getting ready. . . . Silence.

"Well?" said Perico.

"Oh!" said Don Segundo.

Pedro got up and raised his quirt by the thong. "Now you black scamp," he said, "either you tell us a story or I'll make you see stars with this club."

"Before you do anything like that"—Don Segundo made believe he was scared to keep up the joke—"I'd even tell a tale about your pockmarks."

Laughing eyes swung from Pedro's pitted face to Don Segundo's blank countenance. No one knew better nor admired more than I the way Don Segundo, before he started a story, always managed to focus the attention of his hearers on himself.

"I don't know any story," he began, "but I do know about certain things that have happened, and if you pay attention I'll tell you about a country boy who fell in love and all the troubles he had with a son of the devil."

"Get going."

"Well, sir, they say that once upon a time along the River Paraná, where there are more backwaters than holes in a prairie dog town, a lad called Dolores by name worked. He wasn't a big fellow or strong, but he was brave, which counts for more."

Don Segundo looked at his audience as though to drive home that axiom. The circle of waiting eyes agreed. He went on, "Besides being brave, the boy liked the fillies, and late in the afternoon when he knocked off work he'd go down to a place by the river where the girls went to bathe. This might have cost him a good horsewhipping, but he knew how to hide and nobody suspected.

"One afternoon, when he was going to his hiding place, he saw a girl so bright and pretty she seemed the dawn of day. His heart began jumping in his chest like a fox in a trap. He waited till she'd gone by and then he followed."

"A blind man fell in a swamp, thinking he was climbing a hill," observed Perico.

"Sure, and I knew a lassoer who was always in such a hurry that he got tangled up in the loop of his rope. Maybe the fellow I'm telling you about belonged to that breed. . . . The sight of the girl just dazzled him. He followed her all the way to the river, and when he got there she was swimming by the bank.

"When he saw she was getting ready to come out of the water, his eyes swelled big as an owl's so he'd not miss the least thing."

"As bad as a fly buzzing around meat!" shouted Pedro.

"Shut up, you shoat," I said and gave him a poke in the ribs.

"Well, the lad was looking at the girl, dazzled like white birds looking at the sun, when suddenly he got the scare of his life. A flamingo, big as an ostrich and red as the blood of an ox, had lighted near the girl no further than from here to the fire. He kept fluttering his wings in front of her, and she trying to get back into her clothes. Then all of a sudden the bird said some words in Indian. The next second, the filly was no taller than a whip handle."

"Jesus, Mary, and Joseph!" muttered an old man huddled close to the embers, and crossed himself with arms as stiff-jointed as a daddy longlegs.

"The very words of Dolores! And as he had plenty of nerve he leaped from his hiding place, knife in hand, to have a go at the sorcerer. But when he got to the bank, the flamingo was already in the air, and the girl in his talons, huddled up with fright. And it seemed to Dolores that all he could see was a red cloud, above the stream, aglitter as if the evening sun had touched it.

"The poor fellow was out of his wits. He staggered like a sunstruck sheep and fell down, flat as a staked-out hide. Half an hour later he came to and remembered. He never doubted it was witchcraft and that the pretty girl had put a spell on him that he could not resist. It was night, and fear feeds on darkness like fire on wood. Dolores began racing madly toward the ravines.

"Before he knew why or where he was going, he was suddenly in a room where a dirty candle flickered, and face to face with an old woman all dried up like a raisin, who was looking him over the way you look at a lasso someone's given you as a present. She came up close, like she was examining his seams, and felt him all over to see if he was whole.

" 'Where am I?' yells Dolores.

" 'With good people,' said the old woman. 'Sit down now and take it easy, and when you get your breath tell me what's happened.'

"Dolores at last pulled himself together a bit and told what had happened by the river, sighing fit to tear his heart out.

"The old woman was wise in such affairs and she cheers him up, saying if he'll be quiet she'll tell him all about the flamingo and give him charms to save the girl, who wasn't a witch at all but the daughter of a neighbor. Then she came to the point.

" 'A poncho-full of years ago,' she says, 'there was a woman known hereabouts for her evil ways and her witcheries, and she had dealings with the devil and from those dealings bore a boy. The spawn came into the world without a hide, and they say he was so fierce to look at that even the owls shut their eyes when they saw him, lest they get cross-eyed. A few days after he was born, the mother got sick, and the boy, seeing her headed straight for death, asked for a wish. "What is it, son?" says the mother. "Look, Mamma," he answers, "I'm strong and I'll get ahead in the world, but you've made me uglier than my own dad, and how can I grow when I haven't a skin to stretch out in? And the result will be no woman will ever let me love her. My wish, seeing you've given me so little in the way of looks, is for a love charm." "If that's all you want," says the devil's bitch, "you just listen: When you see a woman you want, pull seven hairs from your head, throw them up in the wind, and call your father with these words—" Here she whispered so low that even the wind couldn't hear. "Pretty soon you'll feel you're not a human but a flamingo. Then fly up to

the girl and say—" More whisperings. "The girl will
shrink till she's no more'n two hands high. Pick her up
and bring her to this island and enjoy her for seven days,
while the spell lasts." She'd no sooner finished than death
reined in the witch love of Añang, and the skinless monster was an orphan.'

"When Dolores hears this tale, he begins to cry like
his eyes would melt. The old woman felt sorry for him
and tells him she knows a trick or two herself about
witchcraft, and she'll give him a charm to win back the
poor girl stolen by the devil's son with his foul arts.
And while Dolores goes on blubbering, she takes him by
the hand and leads him to the back room of her house.
There was a cupboard in that room, big as a hut, and
the old woman takes out a bow like the ones the Indians used, some poison arrows, and a bottle of clear
water.

" 'What can I do, poor wretch that I am, with those
three nothings,' says Dolores, 'against the many spells
Mandinga surely has!'

" 'You have got to leave something to the grace of
God,' answers the old woman. 'Now listen to what I tell
you, for it's getting late. . . . You take these three things
I have given you, and this very night, when no one can
see you, go down to the river. You'll find a boat; get in it
and row out to the middle. When you feel you are in the
whirlpool, pull up your oars. It'll whirl you around a
couple of times and send you into the current that flows
to the enchanted islands. And now there's not much
more I can tell you. When you get to the island, you
must kill a *caburé* bird, that's why the bow and arrow.
You cut out its heart and put it in this bottle that's full
of holy water; you also pull three feathers from its tail
and hang them in a bunch on your neck. Then you'll
know more than I do, for the *caburé's* heart, small as
it is, is great with magic and wisdom.'

"Dolores, in whose mind's eye the sweet little brown
girl was forever bathing, didn't waste a second; he
thanked the old woman, took the bow and arrow and

the bottle of water, and ran down to the Paraná through the dark night.

"He got to the bank, saw the boat, leaped in, and rowed out to midstream, where the whirlpool caught him and spun him around like a top three times. Then he started downcurrent so fast it made him dizzy. He was just about to fall asleep when the boat shied to the right and then kept loping along. Dolores straightened up a little and saw that he was moving into the mouth of a narrow stream, and before he knew it his craft was all tangled up in the reeds of the bank. The boy waited awhile to see if the boat would change its mind, but it seemed tethered there, so he guessed this must be the enchanted isle and he got off the pony that had carried him so well, making sure first that he'd remember where he left it so he could use it again for a gallop home.

"Then he pushed into a wood so thick that not a gleam of the star-drenched night could filter through. The underbrush and the orchid roots tangled him up like he was roped. He took out his knife to cut a path, but then he thought it was useless anyway to look for a *caburé* at night and he had better rest till morning. The ground is a dangerous place to sleep, for there are jaguars and rattlesnakes, so he grabbed the heaviest orchid root he could find and swung himself up into a leafy hammock, not without many a scratch from the branches. He settled down with his bottle and bow and arrow, and went to sleep.

"The next morning the screeching of the parrots and the hammering of the woodpeckers awoke him. He rubbed his eyes, saw the sun coming up, and in the path of light he made out a palace big as a hill and gleaming like gold. Around it was a park full of trees laden with fruit so big and splendid that he could see them plainly. He cut and pushed his way, opening a path from the jungle to where the park began. He found some peaches as big as watermelons, and with one he picked he satisfied his hunger and fooled his thirst. With new strength he set out to find his *caburé,* but without much hope, for no one's ever seen this bird while the sun's high.

"Poor Dolores, he couldn't guess what he'd have to go through before he reached his heart's desire! It's the fate of us all. No one would ever start, if he knew what was coming. You leave home on a bright morning; there's a spot ahead and you think it's the end of the journey, you never guess the desolation that's behind every hill. Step by step hope drags you along like a rope till the day you die. . . . But what's the good of talking about things you can't help?

"This boy of my story believed he had only to reach out his hand and he'd get what he was after; it was this that kept him up through six days of suffering! Many a time he thought he'd turn back, and then he'd see the brown girl of the river, and love roped him along.

"At the vesper hour of the sixth day he spied a flock of little birds fluttering near an orange tree, and he says to himself: 'There's where what you're after must be!' He creeps like a jaguar to the grove and sights the bird resting on the trunk. It had already killed two or three of the little birds, but it went on, out of pure meanness, splitting open the heads of those that came near. Dolores thought of the bastard dwarf surrounded by all the women he had bewitched. 'You son of Añang,' he muttered between his teeth, 'I'll take the starch out of you!' He takes careful aim, bends his bow, and lets fly the arrow. The *caburé* falls backward like a gringo thrown off a bucking horse, and the birds rose up as if a string that tied them had been broken. Keeping his eye on where the *caburé* must have dropped, Dolores hunts for it in the grass, but all he can find is some blood.

"He's just about ready to give up in despair, when he sees another flock of birds two rope throws off and in their midst another *caburé*. He was so mad now and so scared that he let fly without aiming and the arrow shot up in the air. Three times he missed till there was only one arrow left. It must find its mark or all his past pains would be for nothing. He remembers that there is witchcraft at work, takes a little holy water from the bottle, and sprinkles it on the arrow. And as he shot, he prayed: 'In the name of the Father!' This time the bird was pinned to the tree trunk and Dolores could pull the three feathers from the tail and hang them around his neck. Then he cut out the heart and placed it warm in the holy water.

"Right away, just like the old woman had told him, he saw what he must do and started down the flowered path that he knew would take him to the palace. A little way off night overtook him, and he lay down to sleep in the heart of an orange grove. Next morning he picked some fruit within easy reach for breakfast, and as day dawned he went over to a fountain before the palace.

"'In a little while,' he said to himself, 'the flamingo will be coming out to get free of the spell that lasts seven days. And I will do what I have to do.'

"He'd no more than said it when there was a noise of wings and the flamingo dropped down by the spring, big as an ostrich and red as the blood of an ox. On hands and knees, Dolores waited, holding back the longing he had to jump on the beast at once. He crouched low as he could.

"The devilish bird was standing on one leg at the edge of the water and looking toward the dawning of the sun as though asleep. But Dolores hung on to his holy bottle, for he knew what was going to happen.

"Just then the sun came up, the flamingo fell in a faint and tumbled belly-up in the water, from which he soon came scrambling out in the form of a dwarf. This was just what Dolores had been waiting for. He pulled his knife from his belt, kicked the monster's legs apart, stepped on his neck the way you do with a calf, and fixed the dirty beast so he'd never again be wanting a woman.

"The dwarf ran screeching into the woods, his groin gushing blood, and when Dolores looked toward the palace there was nothing left of it but a cloud of smoke and a whole herd of little women, each about the size of a two-week-old ostrich chick, who came running toward him.

"He knew the girl from the Paraná at once; he pulled the bunch of feathers from his neck, sprinkled them with holy water, and made a cross with them on her brow. The girl began to grow, and when she was the size God had made her, she threw her arms around Dolores' neck.

" 'Sweetheart,' she said, 'what's your name?'

" 'Dolores. And what's yours?'

" 'Consuelo.'

"At last they stopped hugging and gave a thought to her sad companions, and Dolores freed them like he had freed his sweetheart. Then he took the lot of them back to the boat and rowed them across in groups of four.

"And Dolores and Consuelo stayed on the island, with the joy they had earned thanks to her beauty and his courage. Years later, it was known that they had become rich and had a big ranch with thousands of head of cattle and all sorts of grain and fruit.

"They caught the devil's son and have him shut up in the magic bottle. The evil beast can never get loose from that hitching post, because the heart of the *caburé* is heavy with the weight of all the wickedness of the world."

13

After two trouble-free days on the road, we got to the town of Navarro early one Sunday morning. We made our way down the crowded street to the square with its little church, and stopped at the big store to have a bite. Being a holiday, there were droves of people, and an old pal of my godfather pushed his way over to us with much welcome and reminiscing. I never liked crowds, and less when there's liquor, so I kept close to the counter taking up as little room as I could and watched the goings-on without mixing in. Don Segundo's friend was telling about a cockfight that afternoon and urging him to come and see his almost certain win—he was practically sure of it—over a stranger from Tandil. I put in a dull hour while the country people went in and out, all in their Sunday best; I watched out of the corner of my eye the un- tamed, mighty form of my godfather.

All towns seem the same to me, and all people pretty much alike, and my memory of those stuffy useless places revolted me. When the clock said noon we went down the passage from the bar to the dining room, and here at least it was quieter. We found a shady corner and sat down to eat.

There must have been twenty tables, all told, the tablecloths spattered with purplish mementos of wine. The knives were of some dubious alloy and the forks were bent from spearing elusive bits of food on the coarse china. The glasses were thick and cloudy. A deadly dullness yawned over the whole place.

The waiter greeted us with a smile of complicity that we could not account for. Maybe he thought it too much of a spree for two herders to be having lunch at the Fonda del Polo. "Serve us whatever you've got," ordered Don Segundo. I looked around.

At one of the center tables three Spaniards were talking loud and emphatically, drawing attention to themselves and their shopkeepers' faces. Near the doorway an Irish couple handled their knives and forks like pencils; the woman's hands and face were covered with freckles like a turkey egg, the man had fish eyes and his face had distended veins like the belly of a fresh-skinned sheep. Behind us was a pink-skinned young man, blear-eyed like a white pony; I judged by the look of him that he must be the buyer for some elevator.

"I've seen the pilgrimage at Giles," one of the Spaniards said, "and they're no different from the ones here." Another man at the same table talked with his neighbor about the price of hogs, and the grain agent broke in to give his opinion, with thick German R's.

There was one man who sat alone before a table laden with dishes; he ate, drank, kept silent, as if he wanted to be forgotten for a moment. From time to time he raised his eyes from the heavy plate, and then the bored dining room seemed to be charged with his own contentment. He stopped eating once, long enough to call the waiter and tell him something having to do with a bottle, and slap him affectionately on the back.

In the corner across from us was a team of country fellows who looked as if they had been pushed over there by the noise. They looked on in silence; one of

them had a deep scar over his left eye, both were tanned.
They ate hurriedly and laughed silently over the desserts,
hiding their mouths in their napkins.

Meanwhile, one of the Spaniards was talking about a
friend who'd killed himself. "He came home with a jag
on, sat down on the bed where his wife was sleeping,
pulled out his gun, and right there, before her eyes—
bang!" The other kept on about the pilgrimage at Giles.

The meal cost a lot, but we were glad to pay and get
out into the sun of the street. We rode our ponies at a
walk toward the cockpit, for Don Segundo knew where
it was, and there we turned them into a corral and
loosened their cinches. There were a lot of crowing cages
in the corral, and the early comers like ourselves walked
around and discussed the breed and condition of the
cocks. We settled ourselves in the ring like ducks around
a pool. The judge showed up and sat down by a scale in
front of the pit. The owners came, each with his cock
in a handkerchief, and weighed them in. Then they
picked the spur guards, deposited the five hundred pesos
they were betting, and each retired to a corner to fit
the guards to his champion.

Don Segundo explained the rules in a few words to
me. We waited.

I was a bit bewildered by the moving crowd and the
voices; I looked down at the empty enclosure with its
barrier of red cloth, and up at the five tiers of benches
packed with people, rising like an open funnel.

In the pause before the fight began, the chances of
both birds were argued. The battle, it seemed, was going
to be stiff, the combatants were well matched. They
were of one weight and size; each had been in the ring
three times before, and had come out, each time, the
winner. The public discussed the details of the weighing-
in, trying hard to find points of superior prowess. The
red rooster was not too strong in the beak, which had a
slight crack near the end, on the left side, but he did
have a spirit that the gray for all his liveliness might not
be able to match.

The excitement grew tense as the owners set down

their birds in a fighting position in the ring. The bell rang.

The gray crouched lightly on the ground, his wings drooping like the brim of a bully's hat, his neck arched like a question mark, and his eyes, jet black in a rim of gold, fixed on his foe.

The red was clumsier in his movements; he advanced mincing, head high, and darting like a flame.

A few small bets were laid. Odds favored the gray.

With a swift charge they shortened the distance between them. An inch apart, their beaks flashed in rapid feints; their heads quivered, rising and falling. The first meeting of their beaks made a noise like a whip crack on leather.

The whirls and rushes were stripping off their feathers, and now we could judge their bodies, their thighs, their possible powers of attack and swiftness. We studied them in silence and got ready to translate our judgments into bets.

"Thirty pesos on the gray."

"I'll give fifty to forty on the gray."

The odds seemed to me a bully's insult, taking advantage of a weak point to talk big. The red was aware of his weak beak. I watched carefully. The gray went straight for his foe, closing breast to breast. The red turned a little to one side, and they crossed necks. But when the red felt the blows on his neck feathers, he dodged, lowered his head almost to the ground, and the attacks went over him, without wounding him. I didn't think much of a man who'd put so spirited a bird into the ring at such a disadvantage.

Blood varnished their heads. Beaks sought the ridge of the comb or a torn strip of flesh for the final thrust. The betting, with odds rising, dribbled on.

Twenty anxious minutes, half an hour, brought no change in the fight. My sympathies were all with the red, but he had not made too good a showing, merely standing off the gray's rushes without being able to attack. I wondered if he could use his power, once on the offensive.

My attention was growing subtle. Both my eyes and my ears. They sensed the innermost fibers of these two lives battling to the death so close to me.

The gray kept thrusting breastfirst; the whistle of his breathing grew more labored; the volley of his beak, I observed, was slowing.

"Fifteen to ten on the gray!"

Again, I felt the odds as an insult.

"Done!"

And until I lost count, I kept on taking bets that risked every hard-earned penny of my work. People began to look at me as if I were a madman or a fool. In their opinion all the gray had to do was to keep up his good work and crowd his advantage until he had wiped out the red. It hurt my pride the way they took me for a novice and I grew passionately excited because my money was at stake. I concentrated on the fight as if it were my own, and identified myself with the red rooster on whom I had staked my affections and my fortune.

I thought out a plan of battle. The thing to do was to remain on the defensive, avoiding any possibly decisive blow, to stall at least half an hour and to duck every head thrust.

The red seemed to understand!

Suddenly the audience gave a murmur of amazement. The gray had lost his bill. A small crimson triangle lay on the hard dirt of the ring.

"Now the breaks are even!" I could not help shouting. "Thirty on the red."

But the judgment of the crowd had turned the way you turn an empty tobacco pouch inside out.

"Thirty to twenty-five against the gray," somebody else called out.

I raged at myself for not having taken advantage of the odds to lay more bets. The backers of the gray had become wary.

The cocks were worn out with the forty-minute battle, and each leaned against his opponent. Then my red took the offensive! Grabbing hold of a bunch of bloody feathers, he dealt two hard blows without letting go. The gray cackled like a hen that has been hit by a clod and began to wheel around and around, his neck pitifully stretched out, his breathing clotted with the rattle of blood. The angry little lens of his hostile glare disappeared from his rough, riddled head.

"He's gone blind and crazy!" said someone. And true enough, the wounded creature began whirling in mechanical circles as though chasing an imaginary fly. Then he pecked at the red baize around the ring, turning his back on his foe. All that lived in his empty head was a fiery buzzing pierced through with knife-sharp pains. But no one, civilized or savage, who has not seen it can imagine the fury of a gamecock. Blinded, senseless, the gray beast kept hurling himself against a phantom, while the red crouched, patiently, waiting to deal the final blow.

Weariness, so palpable you could almost touch it, descended like a coma on the ring. It was something that entangled the feet of the fighters, restraining their charges and pressing against our temples.

"What time is it?" asked someone.

"Two minutes to go," said the judge.

I realized that the clock was my worst enemy. My cock was wearing out fast, tripping on the wings and tail of the gray. Then, suddenly, the gray revived, located his foe by touch, and gave him an unexpected blow that stretched it on the ground.

"Fifty pesos on my gray!" called the owner.

"Done!" I answered.

And the red came back, rising strong in his new rage; with a fierce rush he buried his spurs deep in the blind, mangled skull. Slowly the gray sank into the stupor of death, cackled faintly, stretched his neck, and rested his maimed beak in the dust.

The bell rang.

Men, seeming huge by contrast with the fighters, stepped into the ring. The owner of the gray picked up a bloody, limp mass. The owner of the red caressed a handful of muscle, still quivering with rage.

Hands full of bills that seemed tired, too, were stretched

out toward me. I took them, made a thick roll, stuck it in my belt, and went out into the square. There, I saw my red still squatting in the hand of his owner, who stroked him absentmindedly with the other palm while he went over the mighty battle with a group of friends. The rooster began to look curiously about him, returning to the calm of everyday life after the delirious frenzy that had possessed him, perhaps against his will, the mandate of his blood.

Don Segundo took me by the arm and I followed him to the street at the back of the crowd. We mounted and set out, in the golden twilight, for a ranch where Don Segundo had stopped on previous drives.

My godfather teased me about my rash bets, insisting that if I had lost I could not have paid up. I pulled the roll from my belt and counted the bills proudly, holding each one tight by the corner so the wind would not blow it away.

"Do you know how much there's here, Don Segundo?"

"Tell me."

"A hundred and ninety-five pesos."

"Enough to buy a little ranch."

"At least a string of ponies."

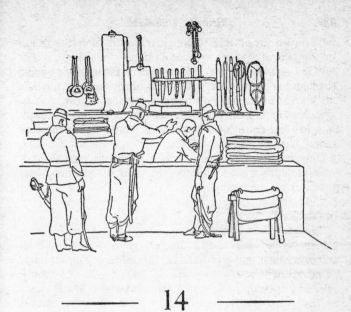

14

Bubbling with good spirits and whistling, I curried my ponies and cleaned up my outfit. The pesos that bulged out my belt made me feel like a magnate, and I spent the morning trying to polish everything I owned to match my wealth. We were going to a fair that was being widely touted by the local auctioneers; I would surely meet a lot of the men who had seen me at the fight, and I did not want to tarnish the fame I had acquired with my bets by looking shabby. At eleven we said good-bye to our friends and set out through the village for the auction grounds. We took a quiet street, galloped through the square, and two blocks off pulled up in front of a store. Bags of maté flanked the entrance, and riding them were saddlecloths, gaily embroidered.

We tied our ponies to the *quebracho* posts that many a halter had worn smooth, and went in. The place smelled of maté, leather, and grease.

The storekeeper leaned alert over the counter like a dog in front of a gopher hole.

"Two packs of Bull's Daughter," said Don Segundo.
"Plug or cut?"

"Cut. A wick for my lighter, one of those black hand-kerchiefs, and that belt over there on the pile of pants."

Like a blow, an authoritative voice surprised us. "You're under arrest, my friend." In the doorway stood the graceless figure of a policeman, whose sleeve showed a meager corporal's chevrons.

Don Segundo made believe he did not understand and began looking all around for the man in question, but there was no one but us.

"It's you I'm talking to."

"Me, sir?"

"Yes, you."

"All right," said my godfather, calm as ever. "Just wait a moment till the boss here finishes my order and I'll take care of you."

This insolence took away the corporal's breath and he could not think what to say next. But the store-keeper, afraid of a fight, got so nervous that his hands trembled and fumbled among his goods and he completely forgot the order.

"The belt is over there," Don Segundo prompted him patiently. "Not the flowered handkerchief. The black one you just had your hands on."

The officer felt himself shamefully overlooked and decided on a show of strength.

"Either you come along peaceable, or I'll take you by force."

"Force?" Don Segundo pondered the word a moment, as if someone had suggested to him the crossing of mules with sea gulls. "Force?" he repeated and ran his gaze of a strong man over the skinny constable. Then he seemed suddenly to understand. "All right, go get your men."

The corporal turned pale, started forward, stopped. Don Segundo slowly gathered up his package, bowed politely to the rattled merchant, and mounted his horse. The corporal made a gesture toward the reins, but halted in mid-air.

"Don't bother," said Don Segundo. "Ever since last year I've learned to ride by myself."

The law smiled painfully at the joke.

In a huge bare room, under a map of the province, sat the chief of police, with round belly and heavy mustachios. "Here they are, sir." The corporal recovered his poise.

"You're strangers?" asked the chief.

"Yes, sir."

"In your town, do people gallop past the police station?"

"No, sir. But we saw neither flag nor shield."

"Where is the flag?" The chief turned toward the corporal.

"The flag? Why, the mayor's got it. We lent it for Saturday's celebration."

"What do you do?" the chief turned back to us.

"We're herders."

"Where you from?"

"I'm from Cristiano Muerto; my partner here is from Callejones."

"Where's your papers?"

Don Segundo had invented our towns, now he invented a person. "Don Isidro Melo over there has them."

"All right. Now you know where the police station is. And next time you forget it, we'll jog your memory."

"No danger."

When we were in the street, Don Segundo burst out laughing. "What did you think of that make-believe cop?"

The fair was something new to me. When we arrived, they had finished cutting out the mounts and were corralling them. It looked like a rodeo. The pen wires scissored the living mass like dough for cakes. Among the corral hands and the ranch boys I saw many a fine outfit. What knives! Silver-studded belts, bridles, halters! Silver spurs and stirrups. The money in my belt was beginning to itch. Under the shade of an *ombú* they were roasting meat for the men and the poor people. There was plenty to choose from on the spits: a side of veal, half an ox, a whole lamb with its kidneys dripping fat.

The organizers of the fair, the ranch owners, and the important traders had a long table inside a tent, laden with napkins, tumblers, pitchers, bottles, even forks. Next to the dining tent, and covered also, was a bar.

My godfather and I got hold of some of the lamb that had been well roasted. What juicy meat! "Shame we haven't two stomachs," mourned Don Segundo.

When their worships at the table got tired of stuffing themselves, the auctioneer and his aides mounted an open wagon and the fun began. He reeled off a spiel of words like "national breed," "matchless future," "big business," and then "opened the sale" with a "most exceptional offering." Around the wagon, either on foot or on horses borrowed from the herders, the Englishmen from the packing plants looked on: smooth-shaven, red-faced fellows, most of them fat as well-fed friars. The breeders for the market, bronzed by the sun, were reckoning profit and loss and nervously tugging their moustaches or scratching their chins. The local butchers kept an eye out for bargains, like boys who wait to snatch a tidbit from a barbecue. The general public, herders and ranchers, hummed with talk about everything and nothing.

The afternoon waned, and nothing happened except that the auctioneer's throat, and my ears, were worn out. They began to move the herds. Then one of the managers of the fair, who knew Don Segundo, told him about a six-hundred-head herd that was going to a big place near the sea. The herder who was in charge of the lot was an old fellow with a white beard, thickset and talkative. He showed us the animals and asked us to have a drink. He rode a white-nosed, dappled pony that I had envied all morning as I watched it work. We walked toward the bar, and I tried to sound out the chances of buying it. If we were going on a long drive, I had to have another horse. But the man talked about nothing but the steers, "Nice lot, sir, and well handled."

At the shed he jumped over his pony's shoulder and

the shiny buttons on his belt clinked as his feet hit the ground.

We walked in.

Our friend went over to an old fellow who was half tight. "I figured you to be here," he said, "and guzzling like a toad in the mud."

"Sure thing. On the shots you serve," replied the old chap with a winy eye and a quavering voice.

"I suppose I was born into this world to support drunks?"

"Shame you never joined the police."

We drank brandy and I brought the talk back to the pony. "He looks a good little worker, all right."

"Look here, sir, I don't want to brag, but I've got me a string of real horseflesh! This one I'm riding today is one of the best and stoutest-hearted of the lot. A while back when he had just been broken I came this way driving some cows for an Englishman named Wales. I had to be on the lookout, for they were wild. All of a sudden we pass a house and a woman comes screeching into the middle of the road to save some ducklings. The herd begins to pile up. 'Hey, lady,' I says, 'out of the way.' 'Why should I get out of your way?' 'Just as a favor to yourself, ma'am, out of the way.' 'To hell with your herd,' she says politely. It made me mad as the devil to see her so bullheaded. I was almost on top of her, and she calling me and my mother all the names she could put her tongue to. Well, God forgive me, I set spurs to my horse, and the woman went sailing into the air."

It was a good test for a horse, but rather brutal behavior, I thought. However, I kept my opinion to myself and we went on talking, and at last the pony was mine for fifty pesos.

We had forgotten the old drunk in his corner; suddenly he started smiling at my godfather, and with a mischievous look, called out to him: "How be you, Ufemio?"

"And who are you?" asked Don Segundo, but I could tell from his tone that the drunk was no stranger.

"Don't know your brothers any more?"

"I got so many in all the saloons!"

"I suppose you'll deny you're Ufemio Díaz?"

"I've got as many names as the days of the month."

"You damn gaucho!" The souse came up to us. "I'm Pastor Tolosa, known as Lazarte, from Carmen de Areco and you . . . are Segundo Sombra." He pointed to a scar across his brow. "Do you remember that? I was the devil with a knife. Now I'm old, and any fool can insult me." He thrust his beard at the old fellow at our table. "But time was when it took a bull like you to gore me." He sat down beside us, and Don Segundo looked at him, smiling as one smiles at a memory, and let him talk. "Do you recall the feast day at Raynoso, when we first met?"

"And how! They told me to keep an eye on you, because you loved the bottle and, for good measure, a fight."

"You kept an eye on me, all right, you sly gaucho! It was you who started things going. A whole bunch got cut up. The whirling ponchos put out the lights. The women screamed and fainted. And you—not a scratch! Those were the days! And then one time when we were just trying ourselves out, for fun, you made me a present of this little bird that sings to me every morning: Ugly mug! ugly mug!"

We all laughed. And my godfather got up and embraced his old comrade, who wanted to keep on about the old days, and it was hard to get away from him. They turned the herd over to us, and with the rest of the men we took the road at nightfall.

A gentle, pretty herd it was! We'd been riding near a month, and not a bit of trouble. Our mounts were lean and alert. Just the same, three days before we delivered the herd our luck changed. The animals were thirsty; we'd missed the water holes and never met a rancher who could help us out. We passed a sultry night fighting off mosquitoes with a fire of green wood that scarcely smoldered. As we started off again in the morning, the whole land seemed to be sweating. Then there came a sudden shower, and the herd tried to stampede. They piled up around the pools of rain, miring the water so all they could suck up was mud. The foreman was worried. He knew that things would only get worse when the hot sun rose.

At ten we came to a ranch. And there was nothing we could do. The brutes sniffed the air and began to gallop down the lane. It was hopeless to try to keep them in line. They lurched over the fences, smashing them. Those that got caught on the wires kept struggling until they were cut or fell on their backs. And what hope was there of stopping them once they got into the fields? The houses were near, and behind a pasture lot sowed to alfalfa was a brook bordered by willows. But between them was another barbed-wire fence and a hedge of cane. We galloped to head off the thirsty beasts. But the fence suffered the same fate as the others, and the hedge snapped and fell before the blind avalanche.

The animals plunged into the water, gulping avidly. Some lay down. The later arrivals walked over them, almost drowning them. All we could do was to keep them from piling up and try to control the tumult. The ranch hands who had heard or seen the stampede rushed to our help. The owner appeared, and our foreman, breathless and a little scared, explained and offered to pay for the damage. Fortunately the man took our involuntary trespassing good-naturedly and, instead of bothering us, had his men help us with the steers, once they had slaked their thirst. We had to cut the throat of one that was too badly cut by the wire, and doctor some of the others. Except for this, everything went on as before until we reached our destination.

15

A fine kind of ranch! Nothing but barren yellow land that looked heavy with fever. It reminded me of the night I had to sleep with my Aunt Mercedes (I couldn't forget those aunts!); she had more bones than skin, like a treadmill mule. But horseflies are better than such recollections!

We had put the herd into a grassy pasture and spent the night at an outlying farm before going on to the coast. What a house it was! When we first saw it from a distance, it stuck out like a dry bone. On one side was a poplar, naked as a broomstick; on the other, three white sticks made a hitching rails. The ground of the yard was so uneven and scaly that, rather than the work of man, it looked as if it had been trampled down by cattle coming there to lick salt when the house was empty.

Don Sixto Gaitán was a man as dry as an alkali bed and as wrinkled as the thong of a quirt. Piecemeal, he gave us information about the ranch we were bound for. It covered a hundred and twenty square miles, and to the east was the sea; but only a man who knew the way could get there because of the crab beds. Inland there was good grazing, but this was far from where we were. A lot I cared for these details. The ranch looked as if it had been dropped and forgotten; not a decent town around for a Christian, not a sign of joy, not a touch of the grace of God.

Don Sixto began talking about himself. He spent long seasons out here alone. His family was over there, not too far from the main house. His little son, he told us, was bewitched; devils were trying to spirit him away.

I looked at Don Segundo to see how this part of the story struck him, but he never turned a hair. The man, I said to myself, has stayed too long on this God-forsaken ranch; he's gone crazy. Then I forgot about it, for I had enough to do gazing at those plains and wondering about the unseen sea and the crab beds.

Even after the best and easiest of drives it's always good to get out of your hard saddle and learn to walk again. I stood beside the hitching rail and studied the white posts it was made of while I shook the wrinkles from my *chiripá* and eased my joints.

"Those are the ribs of a fish you've never eaten," said Don Segundo, laughing.

Don Sixto explained, "More than fifty years ago a whale probably got lost on this coast, died, and was washed up. The owner had the whole skeleton brought to the ranch—for an ornament, he said. Those bones are all that remain."

"Wouldn't it taste fine, roasted with the skin on!" said I, not sure if they were pulling my leg.

"These are three ribs." And then Don Sixto remembered his duties as our host. "Come in if you like. You'll find maté in the kitchen and everything you need to brew it. I'll go gather some dung and bones for a fire."

The thick dung smoke made me cough and cry; I stood it about half an hour and then excused myself, making believe I had to look after my ponies. No matter how bad it is, the open air is better than sitting and coughing like old women around a fire. My horses had wandered

off a way, cautious, as if looking the place over to see if
it was worth buying. They took a nibble at the grass
tops, looked around them and off in the distance as
though seeking some point of reference. The dapple I'd
been riding neighed; the mare raised her head and shook
a shower of anxious notes from her bell. All the horses
looked at me. Why were we so uneasy? What made us
feel as if we needed help? I stood among my horses and
gazed at the horizon. The mare, Mist, sniffed toward the
sea, and we all set off that way, as if we had to.

"Ugly, God-forsaken land!" I said aloud.

We went through a field of bleached, dry hay at which
the horses sniffed disdainfully and with a touch of fright.
I, too, felt a presentiment of evil. We crossed dry swamps.
I don't know why I thought of them as swamps, for they
were level with the rest of the pampa.

"Hateful country!" I said, as if I were answering an
imaginary insult.

A flock of ducks rose from behind a canebrake, as
thick as a charge from a shotgun. The bay Weasel stopped
short and snorted like a mule. We all stood still, more
wary than ever. Behind the canebrake we could see a
pool of gleaming blue about three blocks square. And
birds flying about and crying, seeming afraid. They
watched us from the other side. They knew something we
didn't. What was it?

Mist made a detour and trotted to the water; Weasel
followed. The rest of us stayed behind on the edge of the
field. The black mud around the pool was pitted as with
smallpox. There were myriads of these little openings,
close together, and crabs pranced by them sideways. It
seemed to me the ground was suffering like some plague-
stricken beast.

"That's it!" I said. "A crab bed!" And as I spoke I
wondered why I had taken to talking aloud to myself
that day. Then, as if in answer, the thing happened!
Mist and Weasel in a panic ran toward us. I could not
believe my eyes. Mist's four legs had disappeared, and she
was dragging herself along on her belly! The mud was
opening like waves of water. "The mare's a goner!" I said.

But Mist, lying on her side, began rowing with her four legs, as if she were swimming, so fast that the sinuously wounded earth had no time to close on her. It made a dull, menacing noise until she reached firm ground. "Good girl!" I murmured and recalled the man at Rincón de López from whom I had bought her. But what of the bay? Weasel had pulled up short when he saw the mare go down. Twice he tried the swamp as if to plunge through, but turned back just before he sank, saved by sheer strength. I hurried my whole string of ponies toward him, taking the path the mare had followed, praying to God not to let me stray a foot from the right direction. With a dash ahead, I came up to Weasel, who crowded in among his companions. Then I turned back, shouted "Ahead!" and with the mare in the lead we made for solid ground.

Now out of danger, we went home like children who'd got into trouble, with hanging heads and drooping shoulders. And when we came to the ranch, I thought: A house is a house, wherever it may be and no matter how poor! Compared with the landscape, the place that had seemed so miserable before was now a palace, warm and safe for human shelter.

My godfather and Don Sixto were getting supper, though it was still early. They asked me if I'd enjoyed my trip.

"Beautiful! I almost lost my bay." I told them about it.

Don Segundo answered with a sentence. "The man who goes out by himself should return by himself."

"Well, here I am," I answered self-assuredly.

It was getting dark. The sky hung clouds across the horizon, as a gaucho spreads his colored saddle blankets when he prepares to sleep. Loneliness trickled down my spine like a rivulet of water. The night was losing us in its darkness.

I said to myself, "We are nothing."

As usual, we had to race around doing last-minute chores. From saddle to house, from house to well, from well to woodpile. . . . But I could not get the crab bed out

of mind. The pampa must suffer because of it! And God
help the bones of whoever fell in! Next day they'd be
picked clean. To feel the ground giving way underfoot,
to feel oneself sinking down, inch by inch. And mud pressing the ribs! To die drowned on land! And then the crabs
tearing and picking the flesh—belly, entrails, bones, making of them all a mass of blood and filth! The thousands
of shells acrawl within one, turning the torture of death
into a vertigo of voraciousness. . . . Stop it! God, it
was good to feel the cool earth of the patio under my
boots!

I looked upward. Another quagmire, but this one of
lights. Perhaps behind those myriad holes, there was—
not a crab but an angel? What a maze of stars! A vastness
that made even the pampa small. Then I felt like laughing.

We ate our silent supper from tin plates—hash, of
jerked beef so salty it bit your mouth, hardtack like
quebracho wood that squealed like a pig when you cut it
with a knife. And to make matters worse, I wasn't sleepy!
I stayed in the kitchen, sipping matés. The candle,
weighted by too much melted tallow, threatened to topple
over and the flame spluttered. I straightened it up twice
with my knife, but finally I let it fall lest I yield to the
temptation to give it a smack and knock it over, so it
could light the devil if it liked.

Don Segundo spread his blankets in the open; Don
Sixto was already in the bedroom, where he'd put my
things as a courtesy to a stranger. Fine courtesy to make
one sleep in a place that stank and was surely crawling
with bedbugs!

I put out the candle, poured the maté leaves on the
dying embers of the hearth, and lay down on my saddle
gear in the opposite corner of the room from where Don
Sixto was. I could not find a comfortable position and kept
twisting like meat over a flame, without being able to get
to sleep. It was as though I already sensed the strange
and ghastly scene that was going to be enacted between
the four walls of that God-forsaken hut. Time passed. The
moon spread a square blotch, white as hoarfrost, over the

doorway. I could see the rough 'dobe walls, the torn thatch roof, the dirt floor full of bumps and hollows, the dark mouse holes in the corners. Suddenly something drew my attention toward the place where Don Sixto lay. I heard a kind of groan and the saddle leather creaked. Before I could even imagine what might be happening, I saw the man standing on the bed in an attitude of terror. I instantly sat up, my shoulders against the wall, clasping the knife that was always at hand in the saddle pads that served me as pillow. I drew up my legs so I could get to my feet in a hurry.

I watched. With his left hand Don Sixto made a pass in the air. He seemed to have grabbed hold of something. "No," he said, hollow and hoarse, "no, you don't! You're not going to take him, you devils!" His right hand clutched a broad knife and he made two stabs in the air, as though to lay open the skull of an invisible foe. I had the impression that whatever he was holding in his left hand gave a sharp tug. He stumbled forward several steps. "No, you don't," he shouted, scared but not yielding, "little angel— no, you won't take him!"

The scrimmage grew fiercer; he stabbed wildly and then swung his knife, like an ax, to right and left, his violence greater than his strength. Another invisible tug pulled him to the middle of the room. He screamed, more desperate, "Son! My son! He's not going to be yours."

I understood the terrible hallucination. The man was defending his bewitched child with the sickening despair of one who cannot tell whether he's even touched his foe. What was the meaning of it all? For the third time, I clearly saw the pulls and tugs that threw him off balance. Don Sixto fell to the floor, arose, and fenced with the void again, crying over and over, "No, you shan't take him!"

The incredible fight in which I could see only one of the combatants grew fiercer. The jerks became more frequent as the knife blows and the screams of desperate denial rent the air. The man's strength was failing, while the anguish of his voice became so great I could scarcely bear it. I wanted to help him, but a cowardice, an overwhelming fear like nothing I had ever known, held me down. I could not even make the sign of the cross. The hair behind my temples rose. A drenching sweat washed all the strength from my body. I thought of Don Segundo but could not call out to him. How was it he didn't hear? Poor Don Sixto had fallen exhausted a few feet from me, and there he fought on, his frenzy doubling my panic.

At last, something intercepted the light of the moon. My godfather was there. I heard his calm voice, "In the name of God." I saw him enter, take Don Sixto by the arm, put him on his feet. "Easy, man," he said. "There's nothing, now." I found I could move, and ran to help hold Don Sixto up. Even in the dim light I could see that he was exhausted as by a long illness. "Easy, now," said my godfather again. "Come on outdoors with me. There's nothing now." We carried him into the night like a drunkard.

Don Segundo brought him over to his own saddle, where he'd been sleeping, and the man dropped as if felled. "Let him be," he told me. "And you too. Bring your things and sleep out here."

I was reluctant to go back in that room, but I crossed myself, rushed to my corner, made a lunge for my things, and dragged out what I managed to lay hands on. There was Don Segundo already asleep on the ground, with a saddle pad for a pillow! Don Sixto lay like a dead colt. Sleep? After what I had seen—and not seen! I never guessed you could feel so scared all at one time. Only when day was breaking and my godfather sat up, proving to me that everything in the world was not dead, could I at last shut my eyes. Soon after, I woke with a start. The sun was already warming me, and a tender breeze nuzzled my clothes. Don Segundo had rounded up his string of ponies and was clipping one of them.

Not a sign of Don Sixto! Sun sweeps away fear, and all that was left me of that dreadful night was a dull weight on my nerves.

I walked to the well. The creak of the pulley, the smack of the bucket as it hit the water, the patter of drops as I pulled the rope, and the chill of the rope's wetness on my hands sang familiar cheerful words. I doused my head, my chest, my arms to the elbows. Now I could feel the sun and the wind better. My old strength went coursing through my limbs.

It was a pretty morning, golden-hued and lithe. The desert smiled after its cool siesta. High overhead flew the *teros* screeching their joy. There was a dim bleating of sheep somewhere, and a cloud of gulls, hawks, and vultures spun like a top over some skeleton, there in the direction of the crab beds. What the devil! Life can't stop because some beast or man has had a bad night.

I brewed the maté and went to tell Don Segundo it was ready.

"Good morning, godfather."

"Good morning to you." He laughed. "Is your soul back in your body?"

"What about Don Sixto?" I ventured to ask.

"He's gone to see his boy who's sick. Who knows how he'll find him."

"Why? Have they brought him bad news?"

"Could there be worse news than last night?"

"You mean it?"

I had to get the teakettle to finish brewing the maté. But the enigma of the night before remained unsolved. Why was my godfather so sure that the boy was worse? Did he believe in witchcraft? There was no use for me to rack my brains; I realized that Don Segundo would not answer me, not that morning anyway. But would I ever really get to know this man? Was he skilled in magic too? Those tales of his, did he tell them in earnest? And I? Did I believe them or not? I think I did, because of the way they scared me and because I had little inclination to investigate them further.

I got on my dappled pony bareback and went off for the others. When I came back, I saddled, and with our two strings ahead of us we went toward the nearby pasture where we were to round up some stray cattle the next day. But I couldn't leave without saying good-bye to that ominous house, which was resuming its resemblance to a dry bone. I turned in my saddle and shouted, "Good-bye, you old outlaw! I hope to God a stiff wind comes along and blows you away, with your bedbugs and demons and witchcraft."

16

By nightfall, after we had covered some eight leagues of the same dismal pampa, with only a bite of cold roast meat to keep us going, we could begin to make out the people in the settlement we had been approaching, rejoicing beforehand in its cool green. There there would be, at least, some willows, and dogs, and pasture for our horses, and the owners of the house.

Other herders had already arrived for the next day's work, and we could see one another from a distance among our horses, changing mounts and getting ourselves ready. I selected Moro, the dapple gray, as my best bet for the roundup if I hoped to make a good showing. I trimmed his mane and his fetlocks, saddled him, and set out at an easy lope for the ranch.

We exchanged a few words at the hitching rail with other men, looked over one another's horses, and praised them politely.

"Nice bay you got there," I said to a herder who had

just dismounted at my side. "You'll get plenty of offers for him when they see him in town."

"Small chance." He laughed. "How about your gray?"

"Not bad in the roundup. But what can you expect of him with the trouble he's got on his back?"

"What trouble is that?"

"Your humble servant," said I, pointing to myself.

"That's a good one!" said a lean old fellow with his elbows resting on a stocky dun that stood as still as a bag of wool.

"Soon they'll be telling us how fierce frogs are!" said the man on the bay.

"Keep your eyes skinned, lad. Never trust the cock that comes sidling into the ring," counseled the old man.

A fat man with a face like a half-breed was scraping the mud from his strawberry roan's back with a knife. "That's what I call a horse!" He pointed to Don Segundo's splendid sorrel. Everyone looked and silently agreed.

Don Segundo explained in his even voice, "I got him in a trade for some cakes." When the laughs died down, he went on, "I guess the other fellow was drunk." That is what a good many had been thinking without daring to say so. Don Segundo seemed to want to recall the deal. "What I can't remember," he said, "is whether I was drunk too. I guess I wasn't as bad off as him, though maybe 'twas the other way and I was so stewed I hadn't any shame left. I seem to remember a lot of excitement, even a fight. We had ourselves a time. Next day the other chap couldn't recall the trade very well, but I jogged his memory."

Jogged his memory? They could imagine it was a pretty good jog! Besides, Don Segundo had mentioned a fight—and a good time. They looked him over, taking in the heft and height of the man, and above all the calm way he seemed to take things, as if nothing—absolutely nothing in the world—were more than a trifle. Once again I was made aware of this power in my godfather to arouse in the country folk, as a rule so skeptical and reserved, an unconditional admiration. First he disconcerted them

with his impassive air, making them wonder whether he
was deep or a fool, which was immediately followed by
respect and expectancy. Another art of his was to know
when to stop. With the eyes of the whole crowd on
him, he began to speak in a low voice to the man at his
side.

The owner of the strawberry roan asked me where
we were from.

"San Antonio."

"San Antonio, is it?" the man with the dun broke in.
"I used to work there, on General Roca's place. And
this man"—he pointed to the one on the bay—"was on a
drive there not so long ago."

"That's right. On somebody Costa's ranch."

"Acosta," I corrected.

"That's right, Acosta."

We came up to the ranch house. In the big patio under
the willow, a fire blazed, licking the meat on the spits.
Beautiful smell! There were about twenty of us all told.
Next morning another ten arrived. They came from different farms. There was no doubt that the roundup was
going to be a big one, and hard work.

Nobody cut up or played the guitar or got gay before
we turned in. The people of these parts seemed to have
no spirit. One by one we'd walk over to the spit, cut
off a chunk of the meat, return, squat down, and eat. The
more unsociable ones went off into the dark, as if they
were ashamed to be seen eating or were afraid somebody
might rob them of their prey. The animals we were going
to round up were wild and so a good number of the men
had brought dogs, and as we ate we were encircled by
the hungry, begging pack.

At last the spits were bare. Before turning in I said
to my godfather, "No one's going to drag me indoors
tonight, even if it rains. I'd rather be with God in the
open than under a roof with a madman."

"Well spoken," he said, but I could not tell if he meant
it or merely wanted not to be bothered.

Before day we started out. My workmates were two
big fellows, perhaps twenty years old. One looked part

Indian, tall and pale. The other was fair and skinny, with slanting eyes like a wildcat's. This one got on a white-faced sorrel that started to buck as soon as it felt him on its back. The boy must have felt sure of himself, for in spite of the dark he gave it to him with the quirt.

"Morning air makes you feel good, eh?" he murmured when he had him under control.

The evening before, we had seemed a crowd, but the dark and the pampa dissolving everything turned us into a handful of winged ants. My two companions put me between them. The dark one rode a saddle that looked as if it had been made for a kid brother; his horse was a light sorrel with blue eyes, and wild as a marsh bird. The tails of all the horses were cut about a foot above the shank, the stirrups were crossed in front under the saddle pads: the style of the South.

No one said a word. We cantered along a trail that gradually disappeared until there was nothing but open country about us, with only my friends' sense of direction to guide us. I was a little scared and asked about the quagmires. The chap on the white-faced horse said there were none around that way. Nobody could go near them, he said, unless he knew them well, and they had given us a clean stretch to work in. Just the same, we would have to cross the sand dunes to the ocean, to drive in any animals that might be hiding there. It was all new to me: the sand dunes and the ocean. But I did not want them to take me for a tenderfoot, so I kept quiet and waited; the job itself would answer all my questions.

The first glow in the sky began to drive away the night; the stars fell toward the other side of the world. We skirted a nitrate bottom and a chain of lagoons from which the birds, only half awakened, flew up in fright before us. It got lighter and the pampa began to come to life. We passed the stinking carcass of a steer, with thirty vultures gobbling it up before it rotted away. What a pleasant land whose one joy seemed to be to scare people!

As the sun rose over the horizon, we saw the sand dunes against the light. They were like pimples on the pampa. A bunch of cattle was trotting along the crest of a rise; they saw us and fled. My companions gave the classic whoop of the roundup.

We were soon on ground that had sudden falls and rises. The grass disappeared from under the horses' feet and we rode into the domain of the dunes, the pure sand dunes that the winds shift and often pile into great hills. The early morning light turned the sand gold. Our horses sank in up to their hocks. But like the boys we were we loved it, galloping full speed down the sudden slopes, tumbling into the soft mattresses at the bottom, at the risk of being crushed beneath our horses.

At last we had enough of fooling and decided to get to work. We moved clumsily, at a rocking gait made too soft by the sand. There was not a field of grass in all that bright world that the new sun now softly tinted. They told me that for the width of a league, between the sea and land, the coast was this monotonous flock of hummocks, smooth, brown, unbroken, and so hard that galloping hoofs left only a faint curved depression. What of the sea? Suddenly there was a fringe of blue between the slopes of sand; we came over the last rise. From below to on high rose something like a double sky, but darker and ending, not far from where we stood, in a spume of white foam. It was a smooth blue pampa that rose so high that I could not believe it was water! Some cows were galloping at the very edge and my companions set out after them. I would have liked to stay awhile and take in the strange and mighty scene. But it is better to forgo a pleasure than to be taken for a simpleton, so I too spurred after the beasts.

The wet sand of the shore was as hard as a board and we galloped like mad. My Moro showed what he was made of, and before long he had caught up with the others, despite their head start, and was taking the lead. We gained slowly on the wild steers, which were swift as stags, and as we headed in on them they began to zigzag. They were lean as racehorses, and every time we brought up close to one, it got away. At last the sorrel and the dapple cornered a bull that was lazier or clum-

sier than the rest and edged it on to the dunes. I was
after a brindled cow, and close to her. Driving it toward
the sea, whose roar surprised and scared me, slowed her
down and I was able to get my pony close to her. Moro
stuck to her like a gadfly, and we rode shoulder to shoulder.

Suddenly we struck something slippery and sonorous.
Not knowing what it was, I took my feet from the stirrups. The cow felt herself falling and tried to cross in
front of us but Moro kept pushing her forward. Then, the
inevitable happened. As we came off the strip of hard
rock to the shifty sand, the cow fell and Moro across her.
"If only he doesn't break his neck!" I had time to think as
I threw myself backward against his somersault. At a
time like that, your body thinks and acts for itself. My
feet stung as I hit the sand; I ran a few steps to regain my
balance and then turned to my horse, who was trying to
get to his feet. The cow had righted herself and made a
lunge at me, and I brought my quirt across her muzzle
and sprang aside. Then I got hold of my horse's reins.
My companions had caught up with me. Poor Moro! I
made him walk, and he seemed all right. I brushed the
sand from the saddle and his mane. The boys now were
with me.

"Dirty whore!" I said, and the word sounded good to
me, although I wasn't in the habit of using bad language.
"This beach sure has been worse than a policeman!"

I was up again and ready for work. The brindled cow
had vanished in the dunes. My two mates jabbered away
at me and I could tell that we were beginning to be
friends.

No better breakfast to tone you up than a fall. We
were now ready for the roundup. After a hard gallop
through the dunes we came out to the pampa. Our work
and the work of the others was showing results. The
pampa, bare before, was becoming dotted with steers
that ran in groups or in single file on the side opposite
the sea—the side of mankind, I would have said. Far
away, clouds of dust showed where the roundup was
thickest.

Now we could take things a little easier. The single

heads gravitated together, the groups grew always larger. The steers, unconsciously, were following their own trails. All we had to do was to give them a rush from time to time and pack them closer, and the ground rang with thudding hoofs.

We stayed clear of the fresh cows that glared at us savagely, with a gore in each horn. We made slow headway, for we had to shift constantly from left to right in a tiring broken line. The lowing all about us made a kind of wall of lamentation in the air: the lament of untamed creatures forced to meet their slavish destiny, although they had rarely seen a man, and then only from afar.

About five miles off, on a low bluff, a focus of movement was forming. There must be men there, keeping this nucleus of the roundup in one place. And the nearer we came, the bigger it grew. A growing cloud of dust floated about it and it drew to itself all the strands of cattle which vanished into it like magic. A little while ago the countryside was bare; we were now crowding it with life, sweeping everything toward a single point, soon to leave the fields naked again. Meantime, we kept our eyes on the core of the roundup and longed to get there, for it was no fun galloping after the wary range cattle. Just the same, we kept on and on.

The roundup swelled with the inflowing beasts and with ourselves drawing nearer. The lowing deafened: in the whole round sweep of the horizon there seemed no room for anything but that vast annihilating roar.

We arrived. Some of the men were riding constantly around the frantic herd. Some were changing horses. Others, as they rode, threw a leg across the saddle horn, rolled a cigarette, or chatted. The horses dripped sweat; many were bloody at the shoulders, where the spurs had roweled them; some were plastered to the belly with mud, showing the special work they had been put to. I recognized some of the faces I had seen the day before, and there were new ones.

I watched the roundup. I had never seen such a conglomeration. About five thousand there must have been, big and small, of every shape and every color. But that

was not what amazed me. It was the number of twisted
and crippled beasts; some with fractures that God had
knitted in His own way, others with huge scars where
maggots had devoured the flesh. No human hand had
touched these animals. If a horn grew into an eye, no
one was there to cut off the tip. The ones with maggots
either died devoured or survived, if the weather changed,
with a whole chunk of their flesh missing. Where the
hoofs had spread, they went on spreading until they were
as convoluted as a piece of tripe. The swaybacked learned
to walk dragging their hind legs. Those with mange either
wasted away or were skeletons in baggy, hairless, bleeding hides. And the shoulders and flanks of the bulls were
scarred from battles. For some you felt pity, for some
horror; others made you laugh. The young and healthy
(the majority, for the pampa soon gets rid of the inept)
were so wild it was hard to contain them, in their eagerness to get away.

There were so many bulls of different breeds that the
roundup was dangerous. A number of them were already looking for a fight. The outriders had to keep
some distance off in a huge circle, and this requires
many men. Beyond them, the strings of extra horses with
their bell mares formed a last circle.

"Brother, have you seen the venison?"

The question came from a chap on a small, prancing
dun and referred to the fact that so far we had had nothing to eat. And in truth, we were so famished that any
quadruped would look like venison to us, for it was ten
o'clock and all we had had since two in the morning was
a bitter maté. I looked toward the spits and saw that
the heifer slaughtered that morning was half roasted.

"Why don't we go over," I said, "and do our waiting
with a couple of matés?"

There were plenty of long-horned skulls from previous
roundups to sit on. I could change horses later. For the
moment I loosened Moro's cinch and looked out for myself.

As on the night before, we drank and ate in silence.
This crowd certainly made me want to be alone! As there

was still time before work began—the cutting out of the steers—I left the maté and the company, and went leisurely about saddling my fresh horse. Besides, I needed to get away from the storm of lowings that had just about cracked my head. But why, I wondered, this sudden fit of the blues.

I spent as long as I could saddling the bay I picked as toughest and bravest for the work. I spread out sheepskins, one by one; three times I cinched the straps; and with an awl that I carried in my saddlebags, the point stuck in a cork, I repaired a torn strap. I put on the pads as though I were going to town, shook out my lasso, and coiled it more carefully than before. And when there was nothing left to do, I rolled a cigarette, taking as long as if it were the first I'd ever made.

With that I heard a shout and saw a bull racing toward me with a group of riders piling after him. I jumped astride Weasel, sure now that my blues would vanish. I let them get near, and then I picked out the spot for what I proposed to do. At the right distance I shouted, "Permit me, gentlemen," and tightened my legs around my bay.

Weasel was a glutton for this sort of encounter, and I had judged the distance well. The bull's shoulder and the bay's breast collided at full speed. I put all my weight behind the blow. We stopped short at the spot where we had met. The bull rose like a ball into the air and fell over on its back.

What I had done was the most dangerous game of all. To cut across a bull running at full speed and stop him can cost you your hide if you miscalculate the rate of speed of each animal. A good start for the hard work ahead!

17

The barbarous rodeo began. As there were a lot of us, we did several things at the same time. On one side the bulls milled around the tame ones that were used as decoys; on the other they were headed toward an open field where they were roped, thrown, horned, gelded, cured of their ills, or—if too sick to save—their throats were cut and they were skinned. The fair-haired boy who had been my partner in the roundup that morning specialized with me in cutting out. We took young bulls only, and they were hard to find; after we had driven them into a grassy compound, we castrated them, and then they would be fattened over the winter. But could anything worth fattening be hoped for from that strange reunion of long shanks and swaybacks? We made a smart pair, he on his light dapple and I on my bay. Eager to show off our ponies' tricks, we caught the bulls between us. There was no use for them to try to make a dash for the open fields or to sit tight on their haunches; they had to come along like filling between layers of cake. And before they knew how it happened, they were with the decoys.

My partner was a little tricky, and I had to watch sharply to keep him from getting ahead of me, in which case the bulls might crowd me. But my bay would have let his shoulders be cracked before he gave way in the rush. Then we walked slowly away from the tame herd, to let our horses blow. And this gave us time to judge how the others were working and to yell something at them as they did to us. We all did what we could to make a show of grace and courage. And all in that silence typical of the gaucho, who hates noise and empty boasts. My godfather had teamed up with the little old man on the brown pony. And it was a joy to watch his skill in choosing a strategic point and doing what he wanted with the bulls, making them go exactly where he wanted. They made a good team, he and Don Segundo and his roan, and their work, everyone admitted, was the flower of the art.

But there's never a doughnut without a hole or a rodeo without falls. A man whose keen face I had noticed took after a cow at a swift gallop, grabbing it by the tail. His pony tripped over the beast's hind legs and fell flat on its side. We rushed over to him. The man did not move. Two of us lifted him by the legs and shoulders, carried him to the edge of the field, and sat him up. He took a deep breath and looked around.

"It's nothing," he said. We felt him all over, asking him where he was hurt. He touched his left leg. Someone offered him a flask of brandy and he took a long swig. Then he pulled out his pouch and began to roll a cigarette. We went back to the rodeo.

"Hell!" I said to my partner. "That man had a bad fall! His leg was right under the horse, and he fell his full length on the ground."

"Maybe," he answered, "he likes a lot of punishment. Wherever there's a tight place to get into, you're sure to find that gaucho! If he was stuck into a fenced field, he'd knock his head off against the posts."

We laughed.

But the herd had felt the shift in our attention, and with their old wild instinct flaring they began to mass and to feel out the weakest spot in the circle around them. First they milled from the middle toward the sides; then they seemed to come to an understanding and stampeded with irresistible speed and determination toward a single point. The scrimmage was terrific. The bulls, blind with rage, charged straight ahead, horns lowered. The calves leaped into the chaos, stiff-legged and with tails up. The others rushed about bewildered, charging wherever they could. The men shouted; ponchos whirled in the air; whips cracked on leather. Collisions and falls reached their height; at times horse, rider and bull rolled to the ground together in one mad maze.

A brindled bull tried more stubbornly than the rest to get away toward the dunes, and although I charged him again and again, I could not turn him back. My bay pulled so hard at the reins that my arms ached. I gave him his head for the third time against the bull, but he raced too far ahead and passed him without touching. I threw my weight back, hoping to hold him in, and did not see the danger. When I looked the horned head was on us. I dug my spurs in, but it was no use. My horse fell, caught from behind. I turned him around as quickly as I could, hoping the bull would run past and forget us. It worked out that way, but Weasel was limping. I rode away and got down. The poor chap had a wound eight inches long on his haunch. I examined it, and it was deep. I was furious that the sly bull had caught me that way. Here I was on foot and the fun at its height!

Far off, the raging rodeo sounded like an echo in the distance. I took my bay by the bridle and led him to where the reserve horses were standing, their ears and their eyes pointing steady toward the distant struggle. How still it was here! The decoys and the first of the new herd were huddled together, with three men looking after them. Nobody else, except the man who had been thrown that morning; and he sat there indifferent, smoking steadily, blowing occasional smoke rings. If the herd stampeded this way, I thought, they might trample him, but before that could happen, I would have time to change horses. I got on my dun, Long Ears, and returned to the enclosure. I dismounted near the hurt gaucho and lighted my cigarette in the dying embers of the fire.

"How goes it?"

"Fair."

"Anything broken?"

"Reckon not, just bruised."

"Can you stand?"

"No, sir. My leg is numb."

"Then don't try to move."

"I won't. I'll just sit on here."

I looked over there and from what I could see the herders were getting the better of the struggle with the animals. They had turned the advance lot back; pretty soon all of them would be coming in our direction. I got back on Long Ears and waited.

A deserted rodeo ring is a strange sight. In a circle around the center post the ground was black with dung and urine, and churned by the trampling into a slimy mud that bore the uneven molds of thousands of hooves. To one side, where the herd of decoys stood, the earth was grooved with ropings and with broad slippery swaths, the wake of fallen beast or man. And there too were the skinned bodies of seven sick animals, whose flesh barely covered their bones. Pitiful reddish refuse, thrown close by the ring, and the gulls and hawks already squabbling over it, while thousands more crisscrossed overhead, swooping down and tearing out chunks of the poor flesh over which they fought in the air.

The whole animal throng was coming toward us silently, and it was a sight to see! Five thousand head of cattle mastered by thirty men, stretched out along the flanks. They came closer. We could distinguish the different herders by their methods and their horses. The rebellion was over, and hard charges were no longer necessary. The herd moved like a single huge beast in our direction, carried along by its own impulse. We could hear the thunder of the myriad hoofs, the heavy laboring breath. The flesh itself seemed to give off a sound of exhaustion and suffering. And now they were upon us.

I thought of the wounded herder, and as soon as the animals reached the ring I rode at them and got them moving in a circle. It took a lot of blows and shouts before we had them mastered and got them rotating at last around the mired ring, blindly, as if their running had lost all reason.

On the one hand, we had won the battle, for the brutes were worn out; but on the other, we had lost, for a number of the wilder steers, seeing they could not run, started hooking.

When I got near my partner, I saw that his shirt and the handkerchief around his head were bloody. He laughed

and explained, "We're out of luck today, bo. Your pony got hooked and my rope broke."

To see human blood rouses your own. But we had a right to get mad.

"Let's forget it," I said.

"Right you are." He grinned. And because we'd been partners, I waited while he changed his pony.

The work went on, hard and steady. We did our share determinedly. Some of the bulls balked; we roped them and made them go whether they wanted to or not.

All of a sudden they told us the work was over! They wanted only two hundred head. And all the fuss for that? But everything in that land struck me as queer, and it was better to ask no questions, to take no interest. We hung around for a while, like bread no one wants to buy. The rounded-up beasts could not understand that they were free. The first to leave walked slowly, sniffing about them. In that way they came on the bones of their slaughtered comrades and began milling in a rage of anguish. Their slobbering tongues swung low, their eyes filmed with fear, and they circled around the half-devoured carcasses, snorting with terror. We had to ride into them time and again to make them move.

We piled the wounded herder into a hay wagon and carried him to the house. My partner got down near the fire, asked for the flask of brandy, soaked his handkerchief in it, and tied up his head again. I could see the wound, short and deep; its edges were swelling. His eye, too, was puffing up. Then I wanted to treat my hurt bay, and we went out together to look at him.

"It'll be hard to take him with you. If you're thinking of selling him, I'll buy him if we can agree on the price."

I looked toward the pampa. The beasts we had rounded up were vanishing over the horizon. I thought of the quagmires. I hated to leave old Weasel in a place like that.

"See here," I said, "I won't lie to you. I'm fond of that son of a gun—and I hate to leave him in this God-forsaken place."

He told me he didn't come from there. His name was Patrocinio Salvatierra, and he lived forty miles off in a level, pleasant place. If I'd look at his ponies, I could see for myself how he treated his string of piebalds. It was true and I told him I'd let him know that night.

"If you want," he added, "I'll take the dun too."

"We'll see." I was sad. The day before I had almost lost Weasel, and now I had to sell him! "It's the will of God that I can't leave this country with my bay. Today he's hooked, yesterday the bogs—"

"What were you doing there?"

"Just nosing around."

"To see the pretty crabs?"

"Well, if you've never seen it—"

He was silent a moment; then he suggested, "If it's the crabs you want to see, all praying as the sun goes down, I'll take you, over here close by. There are enormous beds. What you saw yesterday was nothing but a sample."

I accepted his offer, and we went galloping toward the dunes, but in a different direction than we had taken for the morning's roundup.

The country was bare again; hardly a trace of the rodeo remained either upon the plains or in my mind. It had all been a dream that the emptiness of the fields now refuted. The void had something eternal about it. Already from afar we saw the long swaths of mud. As we approached they grew, and it was as if the world were growing. But what a world! A world that had died in its own suffering skin. Patrocinio led me through a maze of grassy islets, and I now felt the crab beds on all sides of me.

"You'll see," he said.

He got off his horse and for a little way followed a trail edged with black and muddy holes as though perforated by bullets of different sizes. And of different sizes, too, were the flat crabs that swaggered sidewise like clowns beside them. He waited till a big one came out of its hole and with a blow of his knife cracked the shell. Then he threw it, legs waving in the air, onto the bog. A hundred profiled rushes, swift as shadows, converged on it; there was a whirlpool of the black circles, with pinching claws held high, dancing a grotesque six-foot *malambo* over the remains of their comrade. Remains? In a moment they drew away and not a trace of the sacrifice was left. But the live ones were roused by this foretaste of a banquet; they began to attack one another, avoiding the onslaughts from the rear and standing face to face, their claws high and their pincers wide. As we stood close and still, we could see some of them nearby. Many were horribly mutilated. Pieces of the edge of their shell were eaten away, or whole legs. One had grown a new pincer that was absurdly small beside its mate, and as I watched a bigger crab attacked him. He grabbed its back in his two claws and pried it open with them, breaking off a piece of the shell. Then he stuck in a claw, brought out a bit of live meat, and carried it to his own belly, where his mouth seemed to be.

I said to my friend, "They love each other like they were Christians!"

"Christians is right," he answered. "Wait till you see them pray."

A few rods ahead we were stopped beside a huge mud flat.

The sun was setting. Out of every hole came one of those hideous hard-shelled spiders, larger and fatter than the earlier ones. The bog was gradually blanketed by them. They began to move slowly, paying no heed to one another and all moving around the ball of fire that was disappearing. Suddenly, as the sun sank, they stopped, crossed their hands on their breasts; and their hands shone red as though stained with blood.

I was moved. Were they really praying? Would their claws always be bloodstained as a punishment? What were they praying for? That a cow or—if it wasn't asking too much—a horse and rider might sink in the fetid mud mined by them?

I looked on all sides; to think that for leagues and leagues the world was covered with these revolting vermin! My whole body shivered.

We went back through the dark slowly and silently. We could already see the little grove around the house, but it was so dark that perhaps it was just a mirage. At any rate we had to cross a canebrake first. We rode in. Suddenly, I saw—thank God—something moving toward me. I say thank God, for seeing it saved me from something worse than what did happen. A bull, half entangled in the cane, was looking at me. I looked at it. Could it be the brindled brute who had horned my bay? I recognized it as it plunged toward me with so violent a rush that I barely escaped being gored. But for the second time it seemed to have caught my horse! God forgive me; I was in one of those rages that almost madden a man. I rode my pony over to a small clearing in the cane, for a man must not go into a fight without a clear head.

"See if it got him," I said to Patrocinio.

He rode up behind the dun. "Nothing but a skin scratch. It must have been the side of his horn. What are you fixing to do?" he asked as he saw me coiling my rope.

"I'm going to break its neck."

It was a risky thing for me to do, and although in a way he was responsible to the owner of the ranch, Patrocinio said nothing. A man of the pampas knows how to look at a comrade and see when his mind is made up.

My anger had hardened into a will that was determined to see the thing through. I had made up my mind to break that bull's neck, and I was going to. Patrocinio prepared his rope too. Good! The common will to kill made us brothers. Men come out of danger undergone together as close as a couple after they have kissed.

Several times I gestured and shouted, challenging the bull to rush me, and as it had more will than sense, I managed to lure it to a clearing. I turned my horse's flank to it, let it get its distance, and with good aim and luck, dropped the noose right over the bull's horns. Now we were joined together, unable to get away from each other, like gauchos tied foot to foot and left to fight it out.

I trusted in the strength of my lariat; the first jerk pulled it to its haunches. Dark as it was, we could see each other clearly. The bull knew now that it was roped, and got to its feet in fury. It, too, felt the will to kill. It looked around, at me and at Patrocinio, who stood ready. It seemed taller, more agile. Suddenly it rushed me with all its might. That was what I wanted. I waited, confident in the skill of my horse. In a flash it was on me. I wheeled my horse aside and tossed the rope again over its head, to be ready for the jerk. He passed so fiercely that Patrocinio, although he knew what I was up to, could not help shouting, "Careful!" But for all my anger I had time to think: The harder you rush, the better I'll break your neck.

Almost at the same time as Patrocinio's shout, I heard a noise like a slap. "It's done!" But it was my lasso—not its neck—that had snapped. The sudden jerk pulled the bay from beneath me. I tried to jump free, but a spur caught in a saddle pad, and down we went together. What a fall! No matter. The bull was still alive. Its neck had to be broken! I had to break its neck! I saw it a few feet off, trying to get up. Its hindquarters were dragging. It looked at me steadily.

"You must have broken its back," said Patrocinio.

The dun got up, seemingly none the worse for his fall. He was gentle, I could safely leave him with bridle hanging. My right arm was limp, and my shoulder tingled like the bog covered with crabs. I understood what had happened: my collarbone was cracked and, probably, my arm had been pulled out of the socket. Patrocinio meanwhile had thrown his lariat over the bull. I groped toward him, thinking dully of my two wounded horses. I had to fight against a growing faintness. Patrocinio knew what he had to do and tightened his lasso till the bull's head lay flat on the ground.

"You're a bad one," I said and pulled out my knife with my left hand. I was afraid I was going to fall. I knelt down. But not yet. I had to finish first.

"Here's a letter from the bay," I said to the bull and buried my knife in its throat. The hot stream poured over my arm and groin. It made a last effort to stand up, and I fell across it. My head, like a child's, came to rest on its shoulder. And before I completely lost consciousness I could feel the two of us motionless there in the great silence of earth and sky.

18

". . . after that, you're to have a good rest."

I tried hard to understand; I felt vaguely that these words referred to me and that I ought to listen. But what did they mean? Who was this fair man whose face was familiar, and this woman on whom my eyes rested with pleasure and who stirred some vague recollection of gratitude? The light hurt my eyes; everything seemed hostile except these two faces. Oh, the pain of not understanding and of carrying a world of heavy shapeless troubles that, nevertheless, were mine! What had happened to me? A little while ago the world had been clear enough —and now I understood.

We were at Galván's ranch, under the bead trees, and the squire, putting a hand on my shoulder, said, "You've seen the world, now, my lad, and you've become a man —better than a man, a gaucho. The one who knows the world's evils because he has lived through them is tempered to overcome them. You keep on. When you've had

enough, your ranch is here, waiting for you. And so am
I, when you need me. Don't forget—"

Near us a rosebush bloomed and a dog sniffed at my
heels. I had my hat in my hand and I was happy—
happy and sad. Why? Amazing things had happened to
me, and I almost felt myself a different person—someone
who had achieved a great vague thing, but at the price of
death.

But all this, I guessed well enough, was not real. What
was real was my bewilderment, my struggle to free
myself of this torpid ignorance. The light bothered me;
far off there were shadows with something moving in them,
making me feel that I had better concentrate my attention on them.

". . . after that, you're to have a good rest."

I remembered something, like an opening in a wood.

"Patrocinio!"

"Be quiet and don't move."

The whole right side of my body ached, and my head
too.

"What's the matter with me?"

"A busted collarbone, and you've hurt your head. And
it seems your ribs are bruised too."

I remembered: the bull, the fall . . . then everything;
the present grew clear. I asked for a drink of water and
looked around me. I was in a big room on a cot. Patrocinio, seated on a stool, was watching me. A strange girl
—and pretty—came in with a jug of water and helped
me raise my head so I could drink. For pride's sake I
would have liked to manage it alone, but for the pleasure
of her hand holding my head and for her tender smile, I
felt strangely grateful and kept silent. The futile struggle
to understand was over. I was happy. And I could not
move.

"Well," I said, "I guess there's still life in the old carcass."

Patrocinio laughed, and so did I. I felt so delightfully
useless that I fell asleep.

The worst was when I awoke. Forgetting what had
happened to me, I tried to sit up. My whole body

shrieked with pain. "Don't move, partner!" warned a voice. And there in a corner, lighted by the dawning day, was the gaucho who had fallen while chasing a cow. He sat on his saddlebags against a wall, smoking and blowing rings. I guessed that he had not slept and must have stayed in that same position since noon of the day before. "Gaucho with guts!" I said to myself and vowed I'd stand my share of pain without a whimper.

"Feeling better?" I asked him.

"About the same."

"Have you slept any?"

"Sure," he lied. "Just woke up this minute."

All of a sudden I noticed for the first time how my arm was bandaged. A strip of sheepskin with the wool inside bound all my breast and shoulder blade, going like a figure eight from under the right armpit over the left shoulder. It was about four inches wide and held me so tight I couldn't wiggle.

"They've certainly got me trussed up," I said.

"That fellow that came with you—he fixed you."

I was at peace; anything done by Don Segundo was done right. What did I expect? With a broken collarbone, bruised ribs, and a busted head, did I expect to feel like going to a dance? Patrocinio brought a kettle of water and for over an hour kept brewing us sweet matés. They put several sheepskins behind my head so I could sleep. After that interval of quiet and conversation, the medicine woman of the ranch put in an appearance. She was old and as dry as jerked beef, and her back was bent. She came over to my side and greeted me as sweetly as if she had brought me into the world. She examined my bandages without undoing them and told me that my collarbone was broken right in the middle, that a couple of my right ribs were fractured, and that the cut on my head would heal quickly. Then she wanted to know who had fixed me up, and said that nothing needed to be changed. I looked at her with eyes big as saucers, for I could not understand how she could know all about me without even taking off the bandage.

She put her hand on my brow and said, "God bless

you, son. In three days, the Virgin willing, I'll be back and have another look at you. Meanwhile, you can sit up if you want to, for you've been trussed up by someone who knows his business. There's no danger."

Without giving me time to answer, she shuffled over to the other man. She made him pull his pants leg over his knee, sent Patrocinio for a halter or strap, and seeing the men huddled curiously at the door, invited one of them in to help her.

"It's out of joint," she announced.

When Patrocinio got back, she told him to stand behind the patient, and run the strap under his arms and across his breast, and hold it as tightly as he could while the other man took hold of his foot as soon as she gave the word.

They're going to rack him, I thought, and it made me sick.

"Ready," said the old woman. And while the one man pulled at the foot and Patrocinio pulled backward with all his strength, she bore down with both hands on the wounded knee. The pain must have been fierce, for the man, who was dark, turned yellow as a new-hatched duck.

"He'll be all right now," she said and advised taking the man home in a cart or on a stretcher, for he'd have to lie still for twenty days. She bandaged him up with a few rags, laid her hand on his brow, blessed him, and took herself off, bent as she had come in.

No sooner was she gone than the girl who had given me a drink came in. She bustled around, smiling all the time, getting the man ready to go. I could not take my eyes off her. What a smart little *chinita* she was! She was neither tall nor small; her face was gay and tempting as a linnet's song, and every move of her body made me jump like a lightning flash in the eyes. She must have known what she was doing to me, for she gave me a sidelong glance and laughed. Did she live there? What a good time and place I had picked out for my fall! If only my convalescence lasted another half month! In a little while two men came in with a cowhide stretcher and carried out the injured herder. I got up by myself and went to the door to see him off. They were settling him in a cart used for hauling meat, propping his back against one of the side boards.

"Take care of yourself," I shouted.

"Same to you," he answered. "Everything's all right now," and he puffed his little rings of smoke to prove it.

Off went the cart, and the men who had watched him leave went toward the kitchen to have their matés. I wanted to go too, and since I felt no pain and they hadn't undressed me, I put a kerchief around my neck and, holding one end with my teeth, managed—although I had to laugh at my clumsiness—to tie a knot. Then I started for the kitchen, which was in a smaller building adjoining the main house. Before I could reach the door, there was the girl.

"And where are you cantering to so frisky?"

"Frisky, is it? Frisky I was, once upon a time. Now I'm lame for a while, and believe me, I hate it!"

"I suppose you are going out to rope another bull?"

"No. But the girls are going to take advantage of me when they see me all trussed up like this."

"Poor boy! I can't exactly see you running off with a girl on your saddle."

She was teasing, but she was giving me an opening! I did not want her to think me a softy, but I could not help probing a bit for her tender side. I asked her seriously, "Are you from here?"

"I'm from where I like it best."

"And where would you like it best?"

"Right here."

"Good girl! I'm from here too, the same way, as long as you are here."

"Lord have mercy on me!"

"Lord have mercy on you? I'm so ugly, I suppose, you can't even feel sorry for me?"

All through this game of give-and-take, we kept smiling at each other. Then her face turned serious and she said cordially, "Sit down on that bench and I'll fix you a maté. You shouldn't run around any more than you have to." She went off, and I sat on the bench and waited a long ten minutes.

She came back with a kettle, the gourd, and a cannister of the leaves. She sat on a low stool and, as though she had forgotten how to talk, set seriously to work brewing the tea.

I watched her with the hunger of months and with the emotion of every countryman who has the rare luck to be alone in a room with a pretty woman. And maybe she wasn't pretty! She had the grace and coquettish airs of the rose of the ranch who knows she is admired. And the charm of her busy hands. She kept mischievously shifting her body, as if to overwhelm me and tie me to her life, like a ribbon to her tresses.

More time passed.

"Things seem serious," I teased her.

"No. It's all going to be a joke."

"Worse luck."

"By the way," she suddenly changed the subject, "did you sleep well at that cabin in the lowlands?"

She must mean the haunted one. "Who is that man?" I asked, recalling the dry gauntness of Don Sixto.

"A good man. And unlucky. We've just had news of him. The night you were there he lost a sick son."

"You mean it?"

"Just what I said. It could happen to anyone, to lose a child."

Then, frightened by the coincidence and by what I remembered, I told her of the madness of Don Sixto. The girl crossed herself. I thought of the song that ends:

> I'd like to give you a kiss
> Where you say "from our enemies."

"But by what miracle," I exulted, "has a flower like you bloomed on this God-forsaken ranch!"

She accepted the compliment as though it were her due.

"I'm not from around here," she said. "I've come with Patrocinio, my brother, to help out for a few days.

There are three women on this ranch, and if you laid eyes on them, you'd not be wasting your time on a God-forgotten little thing like me."

"I wish I were God, then, so I could forget you when I go."

"Flatterer!" she said without smiling, and it seemed without emotion.

"I don't know but—"

At this point Patrocinio came in.

"How's the old carcass, brother-in-law?" he asked.

All the day before I'd been calling him that, in jest, without realizing the privilege this implied.

"Not bad at all," I said. "I don't even remember the fall."

"Maybe. But I never thought I'd get you here alive. You fainted three times on the way. Do you remember the trouble we had trying to get you on your horse?"

"And how should I remember, when all the time I was dead to the world?"

"No, sir. Not all the time. There were spells when you knew what you were doing, all right. When I put the bridle strap around your arm, you helped me. 'Higher,' you said. 'That's right. Just like that.' "

I tried to remember, but I could not. I must have been talking in my sleep. What a long time I had been unconscious.

Patrocinio turned to his sister. "Paula, get going. They need you in the kitchen."

Submissively she took the maté things and left us. Patrocinio sat down, and we began talking horses.

"Well, brother-in-law, are we going to close that deal?"

"How is my bay?"

"Lame."

"You seem to be in an awful hurry to give him a new master."

"It's this way, brother-in-law. Tomorrow I'm leaving for my ranch."

Good-bye then: it's all over! My friend and the girl are going, leaving me in this place like an armadillo someone has brought as a present. How true the saying

is, "You never get thrown at the right ranch." The news
almost stunned me. I did not know what to do; I felt
licked.

"All right," I said, "take them."

"We have to settle the price."

"Whatever you say."

"Eighty pesos for the two?"

"They're yours."

Patrocinio stood thoughtful for a moment; then with a
"So long" he left me.

I got up and wandered about the room. I bumped
against a stool and it made me so mad I kicked it over.

I went outdoors. There was Paula, but I pretended
not to see her. Behind the houses I crossed the shade
of some bead trees, leaned against a post of the fence
that encircled the patio, and looked away toward the
fields. One-armed, lame, even headless, I too was going
tomorrow! I was sick and tired of this unpleasant country, and no devil was going to keep me here, not even
with a three-foot knife. I took off my hat, scratched my
head, and began to whistle a song:

> I am going, I'm saying farewell,
> Already I'm far from you,
> May God keep my house . . .

In the distance I saw Patrocinio driving up to my string
of ponies. Next day, I thought, I'll be going with them.
There's no better place for a herder than the back of his
horse, no bed more comfortable than his saddle blankets. "The only females I need are my fleas," I told
myself.

Paula's voice broke in, playfully, "Listen, man, your
memories are going to get a sunstroke."

I put my hat on and went toward her, eager to vent
my spite on her.

"You'll not have time," I said, "to get out your glad
rags for tomorrow."

"Is there going to be a dance?"

"Why not? We got to have some sort of farewell party."

"Who's leaving? You? You don't look chipper enough to get a job."

Her voice matched mine. For the first time I saw an expression of disdain on her face.

"Maybe I'm not in very good shape," I replied, not wanting to give in, "but I'm going as soon as you folks go."

"Who is 'you folks'?"

My arms fell the way a tired ostrich droops its wings. I could not understand, and I must have looked foolish.

"Aren't you going with Patrocinio?"

She shrugged her shoulders and pursed her lips. "I don't have any boss yet," she snapped, "to tell me what to do."

19

In a couple of days I had come to know the people of the ranch. With the departure of the herders who had come for the roundup, the place fell back into its normal life. We men ate in the kitchen: Don Candelario, the owner, Fabiano, the hired man, and Numa, a tow-headed, overgrown boy my own age. Doña Ubaldina, Don Candelario's wife, brought us hardtack and plates, which we almost never used, for when we had cut our chunk of roast meat, we ate it with our knife, slicing it on the hardtack. Meals were the only times we were together— and the morning maté.

The owner was an affable man, of few words. He'd ask his questions in a gentle voice and then receive the answers with exclamations of surprise—"Isn't that fine! Imagine! I *do* say!"—and his eyebrows would go up and his eyes grow round, as though to make up in that way for the boredom that dripped from his thin, drooping moustache. The result was that when you talked with him, you always seemed to be saying extraordinary things.

"How's the land over your way?" he would ask. "Pretty good?"

"Yes, sir, not bad. Good thick pasture."

"What do you know about that!" (His eyes opened in wonder.)

"But we are troubled by drought."

"You don't *mean* it!"

"Oh, yes, sir. When it makes up its mind not to rain, you might as well start driving out the herds."

"Well, I'll be damned!"

"And sometimes the best you can do is to skin them, as you go."

"How terrible!"

Doña Ubaldina was comically padded with fat and full of fun. She would toss raw words into her stories, like pumpkins into a basket of eggs. Fabiano had nothing to say, but he laughed at her as a dog looks at a roped steer. He would slap his knees in high glee and shout, "Now it's coming! Now things are getting good!" and the rest of us joined in a hearty chorus. Numa was a poor slouch, graceless and dull. He hardly knew he was alive, and if he didn't lose his sandals as he shuffled along like an old cart horse, it was because he forgot to.

In addition, there were the three girls of the house, the ones of whom Paula had said: "If you laid eyes on them, you'd not be wasting your time on a God-forgotten little thing like me." Well, if God had ever thought of those fillies, it was on a day when He was in a bad humor. They were like slabs of dried codfish, and so skittish they never left the house. If you happened to surprise them at the door, like owls at the mouth of their hole, they couldn't get away fast enough or would answer your greeting with a stare of fright. They ate in their own corner, and Paula with them. But afterward, Paula came out, bustling and radiant, and the patio was lighted up with her rhythmic walk, her greetings, jokes, her words for everyone. I couldn't get it through my head that Paula and those others belonged to the same sex.

It didn't take me long—how could it?—to see that

Numa was making eyes at my girl! It was really ridiculous. What a rival! Just the same, I resented Paula's letting a fool like that fall in love with her, and follow her around (though it made me laugh), with his calf's eyes moist and supplicating, wherever she went. I laughed because I didn't know what else to do. I was always running into him, in and out of the house. I told Paula to shoo the mosquito away, and all I got from her was a jesting reproach. "Why, you're jealous even of what isn't yours!"

Well, I couldn't deny it—but why then was she so clever at getting away to meet me under the bead trees at dusk? And why did she sway like a flower in the breeze when I paid her some flattering compliment, and why did she pout when I prudently avoided staying with her too long?

"You're getting shy as a marsh hen: maybe it's the belle of your ranch you miss, and you're trying to make up the love letters you don't know how to write."

A pretty girl is a flirt and leads you on, every gaucho knows that, but sometimes she gets caught in her own trap. To tell the truth, I supposed that Paula rather liked me. So this poor waif began lapping up the poison as if it were holy water. Little by little he learned what had been unknown to him hitherto, and his heart melted in emotions he had only heard about: the love of a woman, the ecstasy of doing nothing but daydream about love while his body slowly mended.

What can a man do in such a fix? What good is a gaucho who lets such desires soften him? I tried to remember my freedom, my strength. But I made excuses for myself. I could not leave—could I?—until I was strong; to try to work in my condition would only set me back. Just the same, I suffered. Many nights I could not sleep. Or I dreamed I was being thrust down a deep well, like a post of *quebracho,* and that they were pounding the earth down on me till my ribs cracked and I could not breathe.

The old medicine woman came back, as she had promised, three days after my fall. She loosened my bandages, and that gave more play to my body. But a man's not much good as a lover with only one arm, especially when every time he hugs a girl he has to groan with pain. Just the same hugs and embraces were all I could think of when I was with Paula at the back of the ranch house.

After ten days of this treatment my arm felt better and my heart worse. I was still all bound up in the strips of sheepskin that served as bandages. The game of give-and-take with Paula was getting serious, and the antipathy between Numa and me was threatening to break out any day into open battle.

All of a sudden it happened.

I suppose my crippled arm gave Numa courage. The idiot began to laugh whenever he saw me, although he could not think of anything to say. He just looked at me and laughed. One afternoon he was doing it a little better than usual, and I took it worse. I had had enough. I told him to get into the kitchen and help pluck chickens.

A fool never does anything right. Numa's face got uglier than I had ever seen it, and he took a few steps toward us.

"You think I'm at school for you to give me lessons?" he said. "I'm at school, huh, for you to give me lessons?"

He seemed to love the phrase, repeating it over and over. Paula, I could see, was worried, but I began to laugh with all my might. And then Numa went wild. My bad arm turned him into a lion! He whipped out his knife and came at me. I sidestepped, and this was not quite what he expected, to judge by the time it took him to change his tactics. Three times he came at me and I began to be afraid that the joke might, after all, end with somebody's blood. I felt sorry for Numa, who was getting dizzy missing his aim so often.

"Cut it out," I threatened, "before someone gets hurt."

Paula also called out, but there was no stopping him now. He was trying hard to corner me so that I could not dodge, and I could see what was coming.

I let him get close. As he made a mean lunge from below, I pulled out my knife, swerved, and gave him a backhand scratch on the forehead, just to scare him. It did! Numa dropped his weapon and stood there with his legs spread and his head hanging, frozen with fear. The cut went white at first; then it filled up like a spring and began to drip and to pour blood. The poor fellow, white as paper, gave a groan as if he were going to spit up his guts, put his hands to his head, and started for the house. He walked slowly, steadily uttering his idiot's moan and leaving a trail of blood behind him. Paula went after him.

I was alone, and I did not know what the outcome was going to be. I felt vaguely sorry, but had it been my fault? Was it not cowardly to provoke a man he thought was crippled? The more I thought about it, the angrier I got. He had forced my hand, and I felt Paula was responsible too. Why had she not scared the nuisance away? "If she wants to walk around with that blackbird on her back, good luck to her!" I made up my mind to act quickly and went toward the kitchen, where the older folks must be.

As I passed the room where I had slept the first night, I saw the womenfolk huddled together. The wounded man must be there. I went on to the kitchen and found Don Candelario and Fabiano. The latter was the man I needed.

"Good evening," I said.

"Good evening," they answered quietly.

"Brother-in-law," I turned to Fabiano, "will you do me a favor? Drive my horses over here, and some day maybe I can do something for you."

Fabiano, silent as always, nodded and went out and I was alone with Don Candelario.

"Sit down," said he, and handed me a maté.

"I want to ask your pardon," I began, "for what happened. You've been more than good to me here and now I pay you back with trouble. It's wrong, I know, but honest to God, it wasn't me that started it."

"Never mind," Don Candelario stopped me gently. "Are you thinking of leaving?"

"Yes, sir. Right away. I've not done right by this house, and I want you to forget me as soon as you can."

"But it wasn't your fault!"

"It makes no difference. I did it. Thank God I'm well enough to go."

I took my knife and began to cut the bandages from my bad arm. I moved the arm cautiously, when it was free, and it seemed to be in good shape. Don Candelario watched me and shook his head.

"Every man follows his destiny," he said. "If it's yours to leave, I suppose God has so ordered it. As far as I am concerned, you can stay on as long as you like; no one shall ever say that on my ranch I ever refused to help a man who has had bad luck. But I'm older than you, boy, and I can give you a piece of advice: don't fight over females."

"I know it, sir."

Doña Ubaldina came in.

"Good evening."

"Good evening."

"We've bandaged him," said the fat woman to her husband, "and he's stopped bleeding. This won't kill him. And it won't stop him from running after every skirt he sees, either."

Suddenly I realized that this stupid affair might give Paula a bad name. I hung my head and I felt very sad. I went out into the patio to see if I could find her. If only I could take her with me! I was ready to forget everything. After a while she passed not far from where I stood.

"Paula, I'd like to talk with you."

She looked over her shoulder, said, "I don't know what about," and did not even stop. So that was the game! I was to be blamed for it all! Was it a crime to have defended myself?

I went back to the kitchen in a bad humor. If a man had behaved as Paula did, we would have settled the matter. Pretty soon Fabiano came in.

"There are your horses."

"Thanks, brother-in-law."

Fabiano helped me gather up my outfit and clothes, and saddled for me.

How lonely seemed the night I was riding into! Always, until now, I had had my godfather and I felt safe with him. But there were seven or eight hours of road before I reached the ranch where he was working. I would be lost, alone, surrounded by the unpleasant surprises these ill-omened pampas had given me.

I went back to the kitchen, and we had supper the same as every night, except that Numa was missing. I tried to swallow my rancor with my meat. When we had finished I said good-bye to everyone, and Don Candelario went out with me. He knocked at the door of the women's quarters.

"The boy is leaving, and wants to say good-bye."

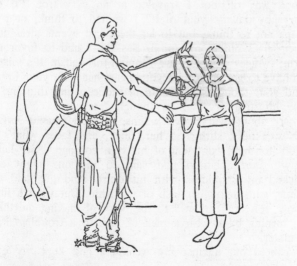

The three codfish slabs came to the door, and Paula. I shook hands with them, one by one; Paula was the last.

"I'm sorry," I said, "for what happened. I did not mean to offend you."

"I don't like folks who are quick with the knife," she answered, stubborn and nervous.

"Nor do I like women," I replied, "who string poor boys along." I said this mostly for Numa and partly for myself. But I didn't want to argue with her, and I added, "Give my best regards to my friend Patrocinio."

"He'll get them," she said dryly.

Standing beside my horse, I took leave of Don Candelario and Fabiano, both of whom wished me good luck. Then I threw a leg across my pony.

Oh, it was good to be on my horse and free! My right arm was stiff, but I could use it. They had pointed out the road. I whistled to my bell mare Mist and the ponies came along at her tail. The same as always. But the night had never been so dark over me.

The ranch where I would meet my godfather was a good way off but I traveled at an easy trot. I'd get there by dawn—what of it? I wanted to think, or perhaps not to think, but to let these last events straighten themselves out in my mind. Besides, I had to favor my arm; twinges of pain were running through it. It's misery to have to go along with your heart heavy in your breast and your thoughts drowning in sadness, and thinking of the injustice of fate, as though fate were obliged to worry about everybody's whims. A good gaucho forgets his weakness, shrugs at hard luck, and faces what's in store for him, confident of his own courage. "Get hard, boy!" Don Segundo had said to me one night and flicked my shoulders with his quirt. And life said the same, with a tougher lash of the whip. But what a hard blow, softening my will to the point of making me think of turning back with a plea of love to a troublemaking female!

I held out against my weakness and kept my eyes steadily ahead.

I splashed through mudholes on the trail, and who knows what they said beneath the horse's hoofs? Mud also sticks to the feet of a man who tries to get ahead.

Unhappy land of these parts, as bereft of tenderness as I! It had a look of death.

The night closed in upon my flesh. And the stars fell into my eyes like tears to be shed within oneself.

20

The night and my journey ended together. As I had reckoned, I arrived at dawn at a neat little ranch just as my godfather was about to go out with a man who, from the first words he spoke, I understood to be the manager. Don Segundo was not surprised to see me; we had agreed that I should meet him there as soon as I was well, and we'd travel north together. My unbandaged arm explained my arrival and saved me from any possible teasing about my ridiculous adventure. I took good care not to breathe a word of my troubles.

We stayed the day at that ranch and left next morning. We spent two nights: one in the open, the other in the stable of a small farm. And the farther I got from that infernal coast, the gladder and more confident I grew, although I still had a bad taste in my mouth. It took about two hundred miles before I could manage a grin over what had happened. It was quite a list when you added them all up: a broken arm, a broken love affair, another chap with his head cut because of a woman, a bad name for knife play, a broken lasso, and two horses sold at a forced sale. This troubled me least, for although Long Ears and Weasel were a couple of good ponies, it was stars and chevrons to my pride to have sold them. What better proof of a good trainer than that folks want to buy his ponies after a roundup? And I did not forget that these two horses I had sold were the first I had broken.

Now at last I had a chance to fulfill a long-standing desire: get me a string of ponies all one color. I still had the money won at the cockfight for this. I could touch my belt and feel the roll of bills. So if it is true that no gaucho ever has a run of luck without something going wrong, it is also true that he can rope a good time out of a herd of troubles.

We had been six days on the road when we came to a country store where there were to be races that afternoon. They had roped off a smooth track; a gringo had set up a tent with food and drinks; a woman selling cakes was already crying her wares, which she carried in two baskets surrounded by flies and an occasional ragged boy; an old man was leading a blanketed horse and offering lottery tickets; and there was a drunk apiece in the tent and the saloon. All these things were familiar to me from the time I was a kid, and I was as at home among them as a frog in a puddle.

The place was filling up with people. Two horses formed the center of a group of gauchos: a quiet and mysterious group, speaking in whispers. We went to the saloon to have lunch. The drunk stuck to us and bored us to death with his tips about the big race of the afternoon, so I gave him a peso with the understanding that he drink it up in the tent. We ate sausage, washing it down with heady wine; then we had roast meat and meat pies. The crowd at the bar was increasing every minute, and outside, the number of horses. What gaucho doesn't bring in his fastest pony in the hope of matching it against one a little slower? My Moro was good to look at and prancing as if all he wanted was the signal to start, and a good many eyes studied him as we trotted past. But I

knew better than to enter a pony that has been a week
on the road.

My godfather, of course, ran into two friends. They
were herders like ourselves and naturally we all stuck
together with that swift familiarity of the shy who find
themselves overwhelmed by the noise and crowd. Both
of them were men around thirty, sunburned and smiling. They asked us what we knew about the races, and
my godfather repeated part of what the drunk had told
us.

" 'There're two ponies you've got to see, friend, you've
just got to see!' " he mimicked the old souse. " 'The
sorrel's won more races here . . . hasn't lost a one except
that time he got beat by seven lengths. And what a nag,
that black one they've brought from the place of a guy
called Dugues!

" 'Right from the start he got the lead on the sorrel
like he was cuttin' nails with his touchhole. And it was
all over. You believe me, brother? It was all over. Yes,
sir. But you ought to see the sorrel, friend. You'd think
he was swallowing up the earth. But, I don't know why,
I like the roan they brought from outside. There you
are. He's got a dark front foot—I don't know why—I
like the roan. There you are. . . .'

"As for me," went on Don Segundo, "I'm going to play
the roan, just to please the fellow. A man who gets drunk
has to be a good fellow."

"That's a hot one! Why?" asked one of the herders who
knew my godfather and therefore suspected there was
more to the remark than appeared on the surface.

"Why? Because when a man gets drunk, he knows he
is going to talk more than he should: and it don't suit a
tricky one to show the warp of his weave."

"You know, brother, that's true!" The one herder
turned to the other.

"Right! And so I'm going right in and bottoms up."

We burst into loud laughter with that nervousness of
the gaucho, who, when he's among people, seems to brim
over with excess spirits.

The races were beginning; and to me they seemed a

way to forget my troubles. The gauchos on horseback
were lined up along the ropes the full length of the
course, like a pair of double bolas: that is, they were
crowded around the post and the goal, and thinner along
the middle. We waited with the patience of people not
used to waiting. This moment of pause was perhaps what
I liked most about a holiday; there was time enough
every day for things to happen, and it was good to know
that for a while, now and then, nothing would happen. The
jockeys were weighing in? All right. The owners settling
the last details of the race, position, weight? So be it.
We'd see soon enough when they brought the animals to
the post and took off their blankets; we'd watch a couple
of heats; then we might find a place for ourselves where
the crowd was not too thick—about halfway down, as a
rule, where the race was already decided, barring a neck
and neck finish.

Meantime, the thing to do was to keep our ears open,
so Don Segundo spoke to a fellow that was passing,
"We're strangers hereabouts, sir, and we'd like to know
a thing or two so we could place our bets."

The man explained: "The stakes are two thousand
pesos. A half mile from scratch, weight equal. If one of
the jockeys refuses to start after the fifth heat the owners
have agreed to put in a substitute."

"So that's it."

"Looks like both sides have brought plenty of money,
and there'll be a lot of outside betting also."

"Good for the poor folks."

"Gives them a chance at any rate."

"Are the horses from here?"

"No, sir. The roan is an outsider. A nice animal and
mighty well trained. The sorrel is from these parts. If
you want to lay money against him, I'm ready to take
on a few bets at ten pesos."

"Thanks, friend."

"Well, if you don't mind, I'll be getting along."

The man went off. Don Segundo observed, "He was
suspicious. He offered those bets because he suspected we
had come with the roan."

"He's sure of the sorrel," I insinuated.

"Bah," said my godfather, "nobody knows except the horse's legs."

I was itching to put up my pesos, and since I knew nothing about the merits of the entries, I had to go it blind. The one sure thing was that the money was burning holes in my belt. I calculated my wealth. From the cockfight, a hundred and ninety-five pesos; from the round-up, fifty; and that made two hundred and forty-five. Sixty pesos from before the cockfight, making three hundred and five; and eighty from Patrocinio for the two ponies. Total: three hundred and eighty-five pesos! Don Segundo interrupted my gloating by announcing the arrival of the horses. We could see them from where we stood.

The sorrel passed, with the jockey up, prancing and eager. It was lean and tall, with strong legs and eyes that sparkled. What a pony! I wondered when I would have one as fine. I'd have to be a colonel first, I figured, for it would not be fitting for a lesser man to ride a horse like that. The roan was pretty, too. Its jockey led it in by the halter, and it came at a long walk that left at least six inches between the print of its forefoot and its hind one. Its hide gleamed like oil, and it was as slender as a hound.

"You never can tell," said my godfather, "but I'm going to follow the drunk's advice."

The sorrel's rider was a skinny chap with a graying moustache. He had tied a band around his hair and kept looking about as if he thought someone might hit him. The jockey leading the roan was no bigger than a twelve-year-old, smooth-faced and sullen as a pampa Indian.

They ran two trial heats. The old drunk was right when he said the sorrel acted as if it could swallow up the earth. On the other hand, the roan ran slantwise, leaning over the edge of the track.

We found ourselves a place. The bets were multiplying. Here was the race about to begin and we hadn't placed our money. A fellow with a beard and a paunch came over to us.

"How about it? I'm putting twenty on the roan," he said.

"I'll take you," said I.

He looked at me as though he wasn't satisfied. "How about forty?"

"Sure thing," I answered.

"Make it sixty?"

The men around were eying us, curious to see how high we would go.

"Why not?" said I.

"Eighty?" His voice grew softer each time.

The others waited. I kept my eye on him and tried to imitate his gentle tone, "Why don't we make it a hundred?"

"Done!"

Already there was a crowd around us as if we were the racehorses. I waited a moment and then, in a voice of surpassing sweetness, I said, "Shall we make it a hundred and fifty?"

The man laughed and then, quietly, ended the joke. "No, thanks. I've about gone my limit."

"They're off!" one of the bystanders shouted.

Neck and neck, not the length of a nose between them, they came up, passed, and flew toward the goal. We leaned over our horses' heads to see them; the crowd flowed into the track. Both jockeys were using the whip. We waited for the shout that tells of the winner, the shout that leaps from mouth to mouth, rounding the ring in a tenth of the time it took the horses.

"Tie!" we heard. "It's a tie. All bets off." But before the crowd could begin its murmurous comments came another voice, the decisive one, "The roan, everybody. The roan by a neck."

"The race was pulled" flew the next news. "There's going to be a fight."

But the word, which bore the stamp of truth, insisted, "The roan . . . by a neck."

I opened my belt, counted out a hundred pesos in bills of five and ten, and handed them to the man with the beard who was waiting politely, without so much as a glance in my direction.

"Here you are, Don."

"Thanks."

My godfather, on the other hand, was stuffing fifty pesos in his pocket.

"I'm off," he said, pretending he was about to gallop away, "to find me another drunk!"

I was furious. Bad luck both at love and at play? We leaned against the wire of the track and listened to the mounting comments.

"He could beat the horse from here twice over," insisted an old man on a chestnut with silver-trimmed gear. "Beat him easy."

The gaucho with whom he argued, a somber, sullen fellow, said low but clear, "Talk's cheap."

"All right. I'm willing to make it more than talk. If you've got something to put up, just show it."

"I haven't a cent."

"Well, how about the others who don't know a good thing when they see it?"

"Bah! You don't have to look any farther than that gray of Cárdenas."

"What can he do? As if I didn't know him! I've seen him lose three times, and if you'd like to know, I've groomed him myself, and timed him."

"Yeah?"

"Yes, sirree, I've timed him with two watches of mine: a regular one and a stopwatch made especial for the horses. And I tell you he's no better than the first nag you run into."

The dour gaucho was out of his depth with this business of the watches and rode his white-faced pony away toward less learned company. There was a rush of hoofs and shouting. We made for the track. There had just been a quarter-mile race between local ponies and the winner rode past, tired and smiling. Now came a heat between a white-tailed roan and a white-faced gray. At every touch of the spur the gray reared in his eagerness to be off.

Near me a group of rich-looking, finely mounted men were discussing the races.

"Why in the world," said the one who seemed best informed, "does Silvano run against that white-footed horse of Acuña's? His bay is untrained and doesn't know a thing. Likely as not, he'll take fright at the crowd and jump the barrier."

Just then a boy came by, offering odds of thirty to twenty on the roan that was about to start, and I took him up just for the hell of it. "They're off!" he shouted. Everyone rushed to the track. "He's dead!" someone yelled; others said the white-nosed gray had gone wild and trampled a number of men. It turned out that what had happened was that the jockey had spurred him till he dashed into the barbed wire and tore himself to pieces. By a miracle the jockey got off with a few bruises and scratches.

Before I knew it I had won thirty pesos. The man who had pointed out the defects of Silvano's horse called, "There they come."

"Let's go watch them," I said to those around me.

What a sight Silvano's bay was! I repeated to my neighbors what I had heard. Then the white-footed horse of Acuña's trotted by, a steady veteran, but rather ugly, a dark chestnut in color. At first the odds were on him. We went forward to watch them start. The bay led in two heats, and the odds became even. The bearded man who had won my hundred pesos strolled over.

"Well, lad, what will you lay on the white-foot?"

". . ."

"I want to give you a chance to win back your hundred."

"Good enough."

The bay's jockey had challenged twice, without result, though they had run six heats. It was apparent that the white-foot's rider wanted to come from behind and overtake him. The rider of the bay laughed, he was sure of himself. Both seemed to want to start as quickly as they could.

Neck and neck they set out; then with a spurt the bay

forged ahead. "Come on!" shouted his rider, giving him his head. White-foot caught up with him. The start seemed to favor him. Rashly, or because he felt sure of himself, the bay's jockey challenged again, "Let's go?"

"Let's go."

White-foot was out in front by half a length; the bay's rider laughed, loosened the rein, and leaned far over his horse's neck. He caught up, passed, let the the other take his dust, and held his gain. Two lengths? Three? White-foot seemed to walk in.

"A fine mess that famous Cárdenas animal turned out to be," I shouted.

The bearded man smiled. "You're out of luck today."

I paid him another hundred. "Let's see"—I was really burned up—"if we can get together again."

"Any time you like, I'm at your service." He pocketed my money. "Just so we don't happen to pick the same pony."

But I did not have a chance that afternoon. I laid seventy pesos in small bets. I held the slips in my hand, sticking out between my fingers like the thorns of a thistle. One by one, I had to pay them off. I went over with my friends to the tent for some beers and fritters that we speared on the point of our knives. Don Segundo was out fifty pesos, but the other two herders had won a hundred and seventy-two between them. I gave one of the lucky ones a hundred to place for me and he lost them on the first try. My whole capital now was five pesos. So that's how it was? In for a penny, in for a pound and I went to look for my bearded opponent, who at once said he would give me a chance to recoup my losses.

"I haven't the cash," I said, "but I'll put up five of my string of ponies. Come and see if you like them."

He accepted without seeing, and to show how generous he was he let me pick my horse in the next race. With the unerring instinct of a lost sheep I picked a loser.

All right. From now on I would watch.

The crowd seemed tired, and it was getting dark. Many, either because they were winners or had been plucked, started for home. Don Segundo would not stop flaying me with his jokes, and the worst of it was I had no come-back. I don't know how much longer it dragged on, nor how many more races they ran. The groups were break-ing up, with handshakes all around. Along both sides of the course riders filed away. In front of the drinking places there were about a dozen drunks. In the distance I could see the clouds of dust raised by those who had left early. Soon we were almost alone.

I took the man who had won nearly all my money to see the ponies. He selected five, leaving me Moro and two others.

We said farewell to our two friends. We were going on and would spend the night wherever it overtook us. I changed horses. Garúa, Vinchuca, Moro, and Guasquita (whom I was riding) were still left me.

"Let's go!" called my godfather, imitating the jockeys.

"Let's go," I replied.

We set out at an easy gallop for the country and were soon swallowed up in its indifference.

21

The day had died away to a bank of luminous clouds on the horizon when, from a hilltop, we saw the old bead trees of an abandoned farm. Don Segundo studied the fence and saw that there was a place where two wires had been cut—perhaps some convoy of wagons had spent the night there and sneaked forage for their animals—and we could get through. There was no sight of a town anywhere; the country seemed to belong to whoever cared to use it; and although there were only four trees, it seemed certain that some twigs or branches must have fallen to the ground, so we could build a fire.

We turned the horses loose in the field, unsaddled the ones we had been riding, gathered dry leaves, sticks, and a few good-sized chunks of wood, and started the blaze going. We filled the kettle from our waterskin and put it to boil for maté; then we sat down, rolled our cigarettes, and lighted them in the young flames of our fire. We had built it near a big log that had been cut and left there, and we had a good place to sit and to reflect that, all told, a herder's life has its good side like any other. My godfather's love of solitude may have influenced me, for, as I looked back on my wandering life, these deep communions with the silent pampa seemed the best of it all. It did not matter that thoughts were somewhat unhappy and soaked in gloom, the way a saddle blanket gets soaked in blood from a wound.

The vast silent land gave us something of its grandeur and its unconcern. We roasted our meat and ate it without talking. We put the kettle on the embers and brewed bitter matés. Don Segundo said to me, slowly, almost

absentmindedly, "I'm going to tell you a story, so you can repeat it to some friend who's having a run of bad luck."

I sipped my maté more slowly.

"This happened in the days of Our Lord Jesus Christ and his Apostles."

There was a pause. Don Segundo let you fall, like that,

into the realm of fiction. Soon we'd be hanging on to the thread of the story, drawn along by it hither and yon.

"Our Lord, they say, was the sower of kindness, and he used to ride from town to town, from ranch to ranch, through the Holy Land, teaching the gospels and healing with his word. He'd take St. Peter along with him on these trips as his helper, for he was fond of him, as he was faithful and obliging.

"On one of these rides (and most of the time they were as hard as a herder's), just as they were coming into a town the mule Our Lord was riding lost a shoe and began to limp.

" 'Watch out for a blacksmith,' Our Lord told St. Peter, 'for we're getting into town.' St. Peter kept his eyes open and pretty soon he saw an old house, with the walls all tumbled down and over the door a sign that said: BLAK-SMITH. He hurried to tell the Master, and they stopped at the gate.

" 'Hail Mary!' they called out and together with a barking cur came an old man, all in rags, and asked them in. 'Good afternoon,' said Our Lord, 'could you shoe a mule for me that's lost a shoe?' 'Get down and come in,' said the old man, 'I'll see what I can do.'

"They went in and sat down on chairs with shaky twisted legs. 'What's your name?' asked Our Lord. 'My name is Misery,' the old one answered, and he went out to get what he needed. The poor servant of the Lord rummaged patiently all over the place, in boxes, in bags, in corners, but he could not find anything to make a shoe. He was coming back to beg pardon of his visitors when, poking around with his foot in a lot of rubbish, he saw a ring of silver—a big one!

" 'Now what are you doing there?' says he, picking it up; and he fired his forge, melted down the ring, hammered it into a shoe, and nailed it on the mule of Our Lord. Smart old fox he was!

" 'How much do we owe you, my good man?' asked Our Lord.

"Misery looks him over from head to foot, and when he'd sized him up, he said, 'Looks to me like you two fellows are about as poor as I am. What the devil should I charge you? Go in peace. Maybe some day God will bear it in mind.'

" 'So be it,' said Our Lord, and they got on their mules and jogged along. After a stretch this chap St. Peter, who wasn't any too bright, says, 'Look here, Jesus, we're ungrateful. This here old fellow has put a silver shoe on your mule and not charged us a cent, and he's poorer than poor, and we've gone off without leaving him a thing to remember us by.'

" 'It's the truth,' said Our Lord. 'Let's go back and give him three wishes, whatever he likes.' Misery, seeing them return, thought the shoe must have come off and asked them in again. Our Lord explained why they had come, and the old boy looked at him out of the tail of his eye, not knowing whether to get mad or to laugh. 'Now think,' says Our Lord, 'before you make your wish.' St. Peter, who was sitting behind Misery, whispers in his ear, 'Ask for Paradise.' 'Shut up, you,' says Misery under his breath, and then says to Our Lord, 'I wish that whoever sits down in my chair shan't be able to get up unless I say so.' 'Granted,' says Our Lord. 'Now the next wish. Be careful.' 'Ask for Paradise,' St. Peter whispers again. 'Mind your own business!' the old man snaps, and then turns to Our Lord. 'I wish that anyone who climbs into my walnut tree shan't be able to get down unless I say so.' 'Granted,' says Our Lord. 'And now the third and last wish. Take your time.'

" 'You stubborn mule, ask for Paradise,' whispers St. Peter again. 'Will you shut up, you old idiot!' says Misery, getting mad, and then to our Lord, 'I wish that whoever gets into my tobacco pouch shan't be able to get out unless I say so.' 'Granted,' says Our Lord, and he said good-bye and left.

"Well, no sooner was Misery alone than he begins to think things over, and before long he's as mad as a bronco because he didn't make better use of his three wishes.

" 'What a fool I am!' he cries and throws his hat on the floor. 'If the devil came along right now, I'd sell him

my soul for twenty years more of life and all the cash
I wanted!' Straight off, a gentleman knocks at the door
and says to him, 'Misery, I can give you a contract for
what you ask.' And he pulls a roll of paper from his
pocket, all covered with writing and figures, in the very
best style. They read it over together, agree on the terms,
and each of them signs fair and square above a seal at
the bottom of the roll."

"The mare broke the rope," I remarked.

"Don't you be getting ahead of the story."

We looked around us at the night, so as not to lose
all touch with this world, and my godfather continued.

"Well, no sooner was the devil gone and Misery alone
again than he felt the bag of gold that Mandinga had
left him; he looks at himself in the duck puddle and finds
that he's young again! So off he goes to town, buys himself a new suit, takes a room in the inn like a gentleman,
and that night he sleeps happy.

"Boy, you should have seen how his life changed! He
chummed with princes and governors and mayors. He
bet more than anyone else at the races. He traveled
around the world and had a high time with the daughters
of kings and counts. But years pass fast at that sort of
game, and now the twentieth was up; and so one day
when Misery happened to drop by his old hovel to have
a good laugh at it, the devil turns up, calling himself Mr.
Lili, pulls out his contract, and asks for payment as
agreed upon.

"Misery was a man of his word, even though he felt a
little blue, so he invited Lili to have a chair and wait
while he washes and changes his suit, for he wanted to
go to hell looking decent. And as he rubs himself down,
he thinks that there is no lasso doesn't finally break and
that all his good times were over. When he comes back,
there was Lili sitting in the chair, patiently waiting.
'I'm ready now,' says he, 'shall we get going?' 'How the
devil can we go,' says Lili, 'when I'm stuck to this chair
like I was bewitched?' Then Misery remembers the three
wishes granted him by the man with the mule, and he
nearly dies laughing. 'Get up, you rascal,' he taunts him.

'You're the devil, ain't you?' And Lili rocks back and forth on the chair staring at Misery, but he could not budge an inch and he was sweating like a butcher.

" 'All right, now,' says the old boy who used to be a blacksmith, 'if you want to go we'll just sign up for another twenty years and all the cash I want.' The devil had to do as Misery ordered, and then he got leave to go. Once more the old boy was young and rolling in money, and he began the rounds of the gay world again. He hobnobbed with princes and magnates, spent money like nobody else, and played with the daughters of kings and great merchants. But the years fly when one is happy, and now the twentieth was over, and Misery set out for his old smithy to keep his word.

"Meantime Lili, who was a gossip as well as a pimp, had told them all in hell about the enchanted chair. 'You got to keep your eyes skinned,' said Lucifer; 'that old boy's a fox, and he's got a pull somewhere. This time two had better go to make him keep the contract.' So Misery found two men waiting for him at his ranch, and one of them was Lili.

" 'Come in,' says he, 'and have a seat while I get washed and fixed up to go to hell in proper fashion.'

" 'I'm not sitting,' says Lili.

" 'Just as you say. Go out and wait in the yard, then, and help yourselves to some of my walnuts; they're the best you've ever ate in your devil's lifetime.'

"Lili was leery, but when they were by themselves his friend said he'd take a turn in the yard and taste the nuts if there were any lying on the ground. Pretty soon he comes back and says he has found a handful and nobody could deny that they were the best-tasting walnuts in the world. So the two go out and start hunting, but devil a nut more do they find! At last Lili's friend, whose mouth was watering, says he is going up the tree to get some more. Lili warned him to watch out, but the greedy-gut paid no attention, and up he goes into the tree and begins wolfing them down and saying every once in a while, 'Golly, they're good. Golly, they're good!' 'Throw me a few,' shouts Lili from below. 'There goes one.'

'Throw me some more!' begs Lili as soon as he'd finished the first one. 'I'm too busy,' says the greedy-gut. 'If you want more, climb the tree and get 'em.' Lili hesitates a second, and then up he goes.

"Pretty soon Misery walks out, and when he sees the two devils in the walnut tree, he lets out a loud laugh! 'At your orders,' he shouts. 'I'm ready whenever you are.' 'But we can't get down,' says the two devils, who were stuck to the branches. 'That's fine,' says Misery. 'All we got to do now is sign another contract for twenty years and all the money I want.' And the devils did as he said and then he let them go.

"All over again came the running about the world and the hobnobbing with swell folk and throwing money around and making love to grand ladies. But the years rolled just as fast as before, and when the twentieth was up, Misery, wanting to pay his debt, remembered the smithy where he had once suffered.

"Meantime, the devils had told Lucifer the whole story, and Lucifer was mad. 'Hell!' he said. 'Didn't I warn you to watch your step because the man was a fox? This time, we'll all go with you so he won't get away.'

"So when Misery got to his cabin, there were more folks there than at a game of knucklebones. But they were all drawn up like an army and seemed to be under the orders of a leader who wore a crown. Hell's camping at my house, he thought, and he looked at the devil's gang like a dog at a whip. If I come through this time, he thought, I'm saved for good. But he wasn't as cool as he made out to be when he walks up to them and asks, 'Are you looking for me?'

" 'We are!' shouts the one with the crown.

" 'I never signed any contract with you, for you to be taking a hand in this business.'

" 'You're coming with me all the same, for I'm the king of Hell.'

" 'How do I know that?' says Misery. 'If you're really who you say, why don't you prove it? Get all the devils inside you and turn yourself into an ant.'

"Anyone else would have been suspicious, but the bad

ones, they say, are lost through pride and anger. Lucifer was fighting mad; he gave a yell, and before you knew it, he was an ant and all the other devils were inside him.

"Without losing a second, Misery grabbed the insect, which was crawling over the bricks of the floor, and stuck it into his tobacco pouch. He went to his smithy, laid the pouch on the anvil, picked up a hammer, and began pounding it with all his might till his shirt was wet with sweat.

"Then he washed up, changed his clothes, and went for a walk around the town. And every day the sly old fox slapped that pouch on the anvil and gave it such a drubbing that he had to change his shirt again and take another walk around town to cool off.

"This went on for years.

"And the result was that in his town there were no

fights, no lawsuits, no complaints. Husbands did not beat their wives, or mothers their children. Uncles, cousins, stepchildren, got along as God orders; spooks and were-wolves all stayed in their places; nobody saw a will-o'-the-wisp; all the sick got well; the old folks did not die; and even the dogs were chaste. Neighbors never argued, horses kicked up their heels only in happiness, and ev-erything ran like a rich man's watch. They didn't even have to clean the wells, for all the water was good."

"Hurray!" I cried.

"Hold your horses!" advised my godfather. "There's no road without a turn, no destiny without tears; and so it came about that the lawyers, the district attorneys, the justices of the peace, the medicine men and doctors —all those in high places who live off the troubles and vices of the people—began to get so lean you could count their ribs, and to die off. One day, those who were left of this vermin were so scared that they marched to the governor to ask for help. The governor, who was of the same breed, said there was nothing he could do, gave them some of the people's money, and warned them not to come for more, because it was not the state's business to feed them. Months went by, and by now the lawyers and judges and suchlike were getting scarce, for most of them had shuffled off to a better life, I hope. At last, one of them, the biggest scamp of the lot, began to suspect the truth and invited the others to the governor's again, promising them that this time they would win their suit.

"When they were all in His Excellency's presence, the lawyer told them that all these calamities that had befallen them were because the blacksmith Misery had the devils of hell shut up in his tobacco pouch.

"The governor lost no time in having Misery brought before him, and in front of them all, he made a speech. 'Oh ho! So it's you,' says he. 'A nice mess you're making of the world with your conjures and spells, you old scamp. You put things back the way they were, and quit trying to right wrongs and chastise devils. Don't you see the world, being what it is, can't get along—not for a minute—without evil, and laws, and sickness, and all those who live by them, and there's aplenty, need to have the devils running about the earth? You get back to your ranch this minute, as fast as you can, and let hell out of your tobacco pouch!'

"Misery saw that the governor was right; he confesses the truth and hurries home to obey. Anyway, he was bored with the world and too old to care if he did leave it. But before he let the devils out, he slapped the old pouch on the anvil and gave it one last good drubbing till his shirt ran sweat.

" 'If I let you loose,' says he to the mandingas, 'are you going to hang around here any more?'

" 'No, no!' they all shouted with one voice. 'Let us out and we swear you'll never see us again." So Misery opened the pouch and gave them permission to leave. Out hopped the little ant and swelled till he was the Bad One and then from Lucifer's body burst all the little devils, and the herd of them stampeded down those streets of God, rolling up clouds of dust like a windstorm.

"And now we're getting to the end.

"The day came when Misery was at his last gasp, for every Christian soon or late must hand over his bones, and this one certainly had made use of his! And Misery lay down on his heap of rags to wait for his death, thinking that was the best way. He was too weary and bored, there in his old shack, even to take the trouble to get up for food and drink. He just lay and gradually shriveled up till his body was hard and stiff as a mummy.

"And then, having left his body behind for the worms, Misery thought about what he had to do next. And, being no fool, he made straight for heaven. He got there after a long ride and knocked at the gate. As soon as St. Peter opened, they recognized each other, but the old rascal figured it might be just as well not to remember, so he played dumb and asked permission to come in.

" 'Hm,' says St. Peter, 'when I was in your smithy with Our Lord and told you to ask for Paradise, you said to me: "Shut up, you old fool." It's not that I bear a grudge, but now I can't let you into heaven when you turned it down three times.'

"Without another word, the keeper of the blessed gates slammed them shut, and Misery, thinking that of two evils one should choose the least bad, went down to purgatory to see what he could do. But, brother, when he got there, they told him they could admit only souls that were ticketed for heaven; and as this glory was not to be his, who had three times refused it, they were sorry but they could not ask him in. He would have to suffer his eternal punishment in hell. So Misery squared his shoulders and set off for hell, pounding on the door the way he used to pound his pouch on the anvil to make the devils holler. The door opened at last, and Misery got furious when he found himself face to face with Lili.

" 'Damn my luck,' he shouted; 'wherever I go, I've got acquaintances.' But Lili, remembering the drubbings on the anvil, lit out with his tail flying like a flag and never stopped till he got to the feet of Lucifer and told him who had come calling.

"The whole damned devils' herd had never been so scared; the Prince of Darkness himself remembered the blows of that hammer, and began to squawk like a broody hen, and ordered all the doors shut to keep out that scalawag.

"So there was Misery with no place to go, for they had turned him down in heaven, in purgatory, and in hell. And that's why from that day to this Misery and Poverty remain on earth, and they'll never leave, for no one will take them in."

The tale had lasted almost an hour, and all our water was gone. We rose silently to get ready for the night.

"Poverty," I said, spreading my blanket to lie on. "Misery," I said and made a pillow of my saddle pad.

I lay down upon this world, but without suffering, for in a little while I was sleeping like a log.

22

"The nicknames of the old blacksmith are meant for me," said I to myself, saddling one of my three horses the next day. Three mounts are very few for a herder. How was I going to earn my living? Nobody would hire me: a gaucho on foot is fit for nothing but the manure pile.

The morning said never a word. The cattle there in those lush fields had not yet come to life; only a few little birds dribbled their faint song like the drip of a faucet. A gray sky, wrinkled like the sands on that ill-omened coast, told of an approaching storm. And we could feel the storm in the limpness of straps, reins, and quirt, all drooping like a turkey's wattles.

Just the same, we had rested well that night and it was good to be moving in the spacious air that tenderly enveloped our bodies.

On we went, following a trail or cutting across country behind our string of ponies, their ears erect to take in every bit of news along the road. After four days we came to a ranch we did not know—a new one. Young trees rose only a few yards from the ground; the brightly painted houses proudly displayed their imposing bay windows and their paths and flower beds as well tended as Sunday clothes. The owner was a young man; he was riding a good horse and his way with the men made me like him. He told us he had about a dozen bays, and if we wished to give them their first gallop, we could have two in payment. Before my godfather could take a hand in the game, I offered myself for the job.

What the hell! I was strong and felt sure of myself. I had passed my first tests, and even if this was my bow as a broncobuster, I would dust off my saddle like I was an old hand. Need must when the devil drives; I was in no position to be choosy. And maybe my luck was going to change. At any rate I had been waiting for this chance. Two bays might be a start of a string of bays—and this coincidence with my desire lent me boldness.

When we were alone, my godfather looked at me out of the tail of his eye and smiled. I did not mind his teasing, and when he saw that I had not been boasting but really meant to do the job, he offered to help me, taking on five of the twelve colts. It was lucky he did! I had my hands full with seven.

I saddled them in a hurry, as in a dream, following to the letter the advice of Don Segundo, who stayed by me and wisely watched over and guided me, saving me from many a blunder. We were to take them in turns; even though the first and the last fell to me, I had the illusion that the work was about evenly divided, aside from the advantage of being able to rest between horses. There were four of us in the wooden-fenced corral. The owner on horseback did not miss a trick, nor a chance either, to help us along with a joke. I asked myself how he would do in a tight place.

As for me, I was scared to death as I saddled the first. My legs wobbled under me and I fumbled over the preparations. Thank goodness, my godfather was there to keep an eye on everything. The oldest of the hands, who was helping us (he rode a thickset yellow nag), roped the colts. We threw them and, while they were still down, bridled and bitted them. Then we tied them to the post with three or four turns of the hitching rope and put on the saddle pads. I kept my eyes on them, watching for signs of trouble ahead. Would this one slip his cinch? Would that one throw me? While I saddled, I had to be on guard against kicks, jerks, tramplings, rearings.

I think the whole secret is a good beginning, for once you've got confidence in yourself you're hard to stop, provided you don't go too far. "Don't go looking for trouble," the owner had said, "but the one that bucks, give him the leather till he lets up." So I took it easy with the first, a white-maned colt. I let him run without spending myself, and on the way back I finished him up with a few strong pulls. "That's one," said the squire. And I felt ashamed, though I kept still. I really thought I could handle something harder.

The bays turned out easier than might have been expected, if luck hadn't been with me. They either bucked straight or hardly at all. I was almost mortified and felt tempted to tickle them a bit. But the fifth made up for all the others. The owner was smiling. Inasmuch as this was one they had been working on the place, I felt there was a catch to it. Why, if there was nothing wrong with him, no trick about him, had they chosen to get rid of him, when he looked like the best of the lot?

I did not want them to think I was an easy mark, so I shouted to the man on the yellow horse, "I guess this is the boy you try out strangers on, eh?" The old man said nothing but wagged his head, and the owner just kept on smiling. All right. They were looking for some rough stuff? Well, they would have it. But they had laid their plans smartly, for as this was one of the pair that was to be mine, I did not want to hurt him with too hard treatment.

He let me saddle him without much fuss. Just the same, I did not like the looks of things. Everyone was quiet as at Mass. When they led him into the field and held him by the ear, I slipped off my boots so as to get a surer grip on the stirrups, and tied my headband tight lest my hair fall into my eyes and blind me. As I threw my leg over him I felt his back arch like a barrel. I settled myself as firmly as I could, and when I felt myself steady in my seat, I said quietly, for this was no time to be showing off, "Turn him loose."

I guessed at the malicious smile of the owner behind me, but there was no use getting mad. For a second I thought of bringing the quirt down on the pony's muzzle but decided against it: I had better learn his tricks first. Luckily for me, my godfather took the initiative.

"Steady!" he said and flicked the colt's legs with his whip.

He reared, pawed the air, gave two fierce bucks, and then whirled wildly to the right, landing on his right flank. I tried to straighten him out, but he squeezed my ankle for a moment, then got up and stood waiting just like at the beginning. I had lost the first skirmish, for my foot was aching; but I had won something too (and he knew it), for he had not been able to budge me an inch for all his smartness. The best thing in my favor was that Don Segundo had already sized up the brute. I understood this when he said, "Don't let up on the quirt!"

Again he lashed the pony's hocks and the bay went straight up in the air. This time the fight was going to be fiercer, with me obeying my godfather, slashing the quirt across the bay's nose and, when he began to buck, letting him have it again and again on the head. The minute he tried to stop, Don Segundo lashed his legs to cure him of bucking. I followed suit and doubled the dose of the quirt, which helped me to steady myself and softened him up. As I saw that I could keep my seat in spite of his bucking, I warmed up and rained a steady stream of cuts on him, singing out like a refrain what the owner had said, "The one that bucks, give him leather! And leather! And leather!" And we sailed down the field without bucking or whirling, in a straight flash of fury.

The game was mine. I had won from the first buck and kept on winning. The reins were of no use, for the animal tossed his head so wide from side to side that he even hit the stirrups. But I kept my balance with the constant beat of my quirt, and I did not lose it till we were back at the corral, where with one jerk I pulled the bay back on his haunches. Then I took off the saddle.

The owner came riding over, and I was glad to see that he was no longer smiling. Instead, he was stroking his moustache thoughtfully, and there was admiration in his voice when he said, "Boy, what a godfather you have!"

"Well," I answered, "seeing I'm not much account I need something to fall back on in a pinch."

"You can take care of yourself, all right," he answered. "But that man—he's not like any of the rest of us."

We finished the job in silence. The last colt kicked up a little, but after what I had been through it was child's play. We tied the twelve to the hitching rail with stout halters and made for the house. A wrangler's work has its compensations, thank God. While the rest of the men were hard at work in the fields, at ten in the morning, we had already earned the right to sit around drinking matés, mending our thongs and saddles, and taking orders from no one.

My ankle had swelled a little and hurt, so I went around to the well outside the kitchen, pulled up a bucket of water, peeled off my shoe and sock, and began to pour pitchers of water over it. The cool water helped some, and I sat on, my body aching, with no thought but to keep on bathing the hurt for a long time. I could see the big barn, the path that led from it to the well, the corrals some distance away, the young casuarina trees that made the beginning of a grove, their tops asway in the breeze, and a little black-polled bird that came blithely near to drink from the rivulet formed by the drippings of my bucket. Then I saw the man who had helped us to rope colts that morning come up the path from the barn.

He stopped in front of me. "I have a message for you."

"I am listening."

"Is this your work?"

"Is what my work?"

"Breaking ponies."

"No, sir, I'm a herder. Only, when there's a chance, now and then, to pick up a bargain."

"How'd you like to stay on here as wrangler? The boss told me to ask you. I'm getting old, I've been at the job for thirty years. Up till now, when they needed a wrangler, they brought him in while there was work to do and then let him go. The boss did not want to keep one steady."

We walked toward the stables. I was flattered by the offer, but it seemed impossible to live apart from my godfather.

"Is the offer just for me?"

"Just for you."

I spread my saddle gear to air in the shade of the barn's eaves. Don Segundo wasn't around. After a while the owner came over and said to the old man, "Well?"

"He hasn't decided yet. I've given him your message."

"What's your name?" the owner asked me.

"I wish I knew, sir."

He frowned. "Don't you know, either, where you're from?"

"What does all this mean?" I said to myself.

"So you don't even want to tell the names of your parents?"

"Parents! I'm the child of hard knocks; that's all the family I've got. Where I come from, folks used to call me the *guacho*."

The man tugged at his moustache and looked me straight in the face. I'd never been looked over so steadily before.

"All the more reason," he said, "why you should stay with me."

"I'm really sorry, sir, but I've got engagements I can't break. You'll excuse me—and many thanks just the same."

The man went off.

The old wrangler sat down with me under the eaves. It must have been a day made for giving advice, for the old fellow pensively thrashed the ground with his quirt for a while and then said, "See here, boy, I don't want to meddle in your affairs, but you shouldn't pass up a chance like this without first thinking it over. The owner can be kind when he wants to, even though he's a bit bossy about the work. More than one man has left here, I can tell you, with his own string of ponies or flock of sheep. I, though I've worked hard enough for it, have enough salted away for my old age and my cubs. When the time comes, I tell you, Don Juan knows how to be generous. He opens his hand wide, and the pesos slip through."

"Look, Don," I answered right off, "I don't mean to belittle anyone, and I know what goodwill is worth; but you see that man over there?" Don Segundo was coming through the yard, his little hat on his head, his familiar *chiripá* slowly dragging, and a couple of lassos rolled up in his arm. "Well, sir, he too has a big hand—even bigger, God help us, when it holds a knife—and he can open it wide, just like your boss; but what's in it aren't pieces of gold but the real things of life."

The wrangler got up, gave me a slap on the shoulder, and walked silently away. I felt sheepish. What the devil did it all mean, their wanting me to stay, and slapping me on the back, and treating me with so much consideration?

23

That tricky horse I had broken gave me trouble enough, and with my swollen foot, more than once I felt that I had made a bad deal; but I was upheld by the satisfaction of having come through the test and made a good job of the horse-breaking. It seemed, from what the men said, that I had succeeded in making that particular horse knuckle under when many others had failed. I don't think I'm more vain than anyone else—who is not vulnerable to praise?—but the pride of conquest, the gaucho's great and steady task, gave me a vigor based on self-confidence.

What a will to conquer there must be in a man to put him through the long hours of untiring effort for a moment of victory! To come out of a tussle with a bucking horse (and the bridling of your own fears and doubts) carries with it hours of nervous tension. Victory is a bright instant, but wearing are the tasks of slowly gentling the animals, of keeping them from picking up bad habits, of correcting those they already have by instinct.

True, I was practically an instrument in the hands of my godfather, who guided every move I made, but it was the instrument that had to endure the heavy gallops of the colts, their sharp halts, the stubborn willfulness of their stupid, untrained necks, their attempts to kick, their jerks when I went to bridle them, and the clumsy shyings when I got on or off, their sudden flareups, which ended in bucking or pitching.

I went through it all like a man asleep. Fixed ideas pursued me like commands in the voice of my godfather. And that voice was as close and constant, even when he was not there, as if it had been my own! When I lay down to rest, his teachings buzzed on in my brain like a swarm of wasps too big for the nest they were trying to crowd into. I was aware of my own passiveness, and it might have troubled me, had not my very desire for independence kept saying, "Never mind, in time you'll be able to do all this by yourself."

As the animals got gentler, we lengthened our rides until we were going as far as a wayside saloon that stood at the ford of a brook, about seven miles from the ranch. And meantime I had made a friend on the ranch. His name was Antenor Barragán, a tall and slender fellow, amazingly agile and strong. He was famed all over the country as a wrestler, and he showed off his unconquerable skill whenever there was occasion. On the ranch he was jack-of-all-trades: it was all one to him whether he rode a new-broken colt or dropped bareback on a pony from a gate or toiled afoot in the corral. He could leap from the ground to the back of any horse, lift any weight. And his gay, dark face won him immediate liking, and his kindness, real friendship. Just the same, all in fun, he'd often rock a friend back on his heels with a good-natured slap. He would make me tell him about my days as a town loafer, and then in turn he'd treat me to a tale of his own pranks, which were never bad-intentioned. He liked to get himself in a tight place to see how he could get out.

Before long we were like brothers. Poor Antenor! Where is he now, I wonder?

When our colts at last were completely broken and used to the bit, we came out of the ranch office with a few more pesos in our belt and took our leave of the owner and the men. It was a Sunday. Custom and courtesy demanded that we stop at the saloon by the brook and stand drinks. There was quite a crowd— plenty of men on the playing field and not a few customers at the bar.

We said hello all around and then my godfather excused himself to pay a visit to his friend the owner. I should explain that the saloonkeeper never used to serve us at the bar, but always invited us into a little inner room, as a mark of attention. As we were going through the door, one of the men stopped us and warned us not to do the usual thing that day, as the owner was tight and he was not a man who carried his liquor well. Others chimed in with the same advice, but Don Segundo said a friend was a friend, and knocked at the door. I followed.

A boy stared at us, amazed at our boldness.

"I'll tell Dad," he said at last. And Dad appeared, with a face like the Last Judgment. He didn't answer our greetings.

"What you fellows want?" he bellowed like a bull.

Don Segundo went up close to him, looking him straight in the eyes, which were watery and bright, and answered, with his mocking courtesy, "I'd like a glass of brandy."

"What kind?" The drunken man seemed to lunge offensively with his words. "The kind everybody drinks?"

Don Segundo winked at me, came breast to breast with the bully, and then gently, as though correcting an innocent mistake, he said, "Of course, not! The brand *you* drink."

That finished it. The man who was rough in his cups put his insolence in his pocket for a better occasion and poured out a couple of drinks.

"Oh, you must have one with us," said Don Segundo,

polite as ever. And we all drank to our future happiness, draining the glasses.

We went back among the crowd, and my godfather shook his head. "I'm sorry for his wife. Sure as fate, the scamp'll take it out on her."

One of the first persons I saw when we came out was Antenor. He invited us to have a drink and we strolled over to the bar. I was telling about the run-in with the owner, when a strange man came up, shook hands all around, and began talking in a loud voice to everybody. He must have been about fifty, dressed like a gaucho, and he carried a long knife with a silver handle in a silver sheath. His brown poncho was thrown across his shoulder, and to judge by his muddied, sweaty boots, his horse, his appearance, and the way he walked, he seemed to have come from a long way off.

He invited the whole crowd up to the bar, and pretty soon with that and his jokes he had become what he seemed to want to be: the center of attention. Suddenly, he began to talk to Antenor as if he knew him, making pointed reference to his strength and skill as a wrestler. But so oblique and roundabout was his praise that it was a long time before we saw what he was driving at. Then all at once it became clear that he was trying to pick a fight.

"I wonder," he said, "just the same, if the lad's blood might not curdle if he found himself looking at a knife."

As if we all were asking the same question, we turned to Antenor. He was pale and kept his eyes down. He seemed scared.

"I, too," the man with the gray moustache went on, "was a fighter when I was young. Even now, I believe I could put my mark on this lad anywhere I liked."

Antenor raised his head, and still giving us the painful feeling that he was afraid, answered, "Sir, I'm a peaceable person, and though I wrestle for fun, I'm not looking to trouble anyone and I want no one to trouble me."

"Listen to him! Tender as a squab!" jeered the man. "And at that," he said, turning to the crowd, "I wasn't going to spoil his looks; just at most draw a little blood so the two of us could test our eyesight. But I'm afraid his eye has gone a bit cloudy all of a sudden."

"May I say a word?" my godfather broke in unexpectedly.

"Why not?" said the stranger.

Don Segundo turned to Antenor. "See here, boy," he said while everyone, and I most of all, looked on in amazement, "for quite a while now this gentleman has been inviting you, as polite as could be, and you're missing the chance to have a little fun."

What was the quarrelsome stranger going to say to that?

For a moment he was silent. Then, more serious, as he understood that someone else might take up his challenge, he gave us a clue to the real situation. "I'm not looking for fun. That would be showing off like a gamecock, when a fellow thinks he can have everything his own way."

Now it was clear: there was a grudge beneath the fire-eating words of the gaucho.

And what about Antenor?

He straightened up and looked the other in the eye, and we understood one thing more. He knew what—and whom—it was all about.

"I was nothing but a kid," he said grimly. "And she was a bitch who went with any man that snapped his fingers at her. At the ranch we called her 'the one you learn on.' "

The stranger made a furious rush at him. The nearest men held him back. Antenor, still pale but perhaps with anger, said, "Let's go outside where there's more room."

We followed. Alongside the door the stranger took off his spurs, rolled his poncho around his left arm as a shield, and drew his knife leisurely. It was as if he had forgotten his recent rage. He smiled disdainfully. "Now you're going to see how a long-tongued calf gets his muzzle cut."

There was a wagon in the yard. Antenor stood with his back against one of the big wheels and waited. The

stranger confidently came forward, and as if he were
playing with a child, flicked the fringe of his poncho in
the other's face. Antenor veered slightly, and the poncho
did not touch him. The pass was perfect in precision:
not an inch more or less than was needed. We must all
have had one thought when we saw it: poor old gaucho!
He'll pay for his big talk. The man closed in. Antenor,
steady, with only a work knife against a poignard and
no poncho to shield him, foiled every rush with a slight
movement of his body. Suddenly he thrust his armed
hand forward and leaped the distance between them; the
gaucho's face was slashed from moustache to ear.
Antenor backed away to show that the fight was over.
Men moved between them.

"Stand aside," said the stranger. "Only one of us is
coming out of this!"

Antenor left the shelter of the cart, where he had
fought with mere shifts of his body. Light and tense, he
moved in to clean up the quarrel he had not sought.

It did not take long. They came together, and we saw
the man rise in the air as high as Antenor and then
fall back like a rag. That was the end. We picked him
up and sat him on the ground against the wall of the
saloon. The blood was gushing from his breast. We
formed a circle around him. And in futile anguish we
watched the advance of death into the body with every
breath, irresistibly driving life out in a flood of blood
and fever.

The man, who had turned the color of clay, managed
to murmur faintly, "The police'll be coming for this lad.
You all are witnesses that I started it."

Antenor was already on his horse and fleeing.

His abdomen and legs drenched red, the man began
to grow stiff.

Someone cried in a fury, "Shit! We pretend we're
Christians and we're dogs—dogs!"

Another, calmer and more thoughtful, said, "Pride is
what kills us. When a man insults us, the best thing we
could do would be to pay no attention. But no! We're
proud. We've got to talk louder than anyone else, and

one word leads to another and at last all that's left is the knife."

"Yes, sir. We're a pack of dogs, and yet we go around calling ourselves Christians."

"I've had my share of these quarrels," my godfather spoke up, "and with bad men too, or men who thought they were bad. But I've never been cut nor needed to kill anybody. I didn't have to, that's all. But the poor lad was not to blame. The fight was fair and according to the man's challenge. Just the same, it should have ended with the first cut."

"And over females," said another. "Over a female I knew, and she's a bitch just like the boy said. And not young, either. Well, it's fate. The man was looking for it."

He lay there, dead, to prove it, his eyes wide open and his body freed of all cares. They threw a blanket over him to keep away the flies.

We waited around drearily until the police arrived with a doctor. He went up to the corpse and lifted the blanket. He examined him, and then he spoke words that I have stored in my memory although I did not understand them until years later.

"What a knife cut! When I was a student, and I was no weakling either, I had to sweat half an hour to open a thorax like that!"

The drunken saloonkeeper had not come out.

We left the job of disposing of the corpse to the police and took our leave.

24

That brutal scene I had witnessed gave me much to ponder over. To think that a lighthearted peaceable man like Antenor should be forced first to fight, and then to kill, was terrifying! Then a man is not master even of his own person? Any chance meeting may play the part of fate and shatter the very foundations of one's life? Are we what we believe ourselves to be, or do we accept things like clues that reveal us to ourselves? I went over my own life, and my godfather's, and that of all the persons I knew. Only Don Segundo seemed to escape the fatal law that buffets us about and makes us dance to the tune it sets. Suppose I had cut Numa's throat instead of merely scratching his forehead? Suppose Paula had let me make love to her? Or, going back still further, what if I hadn't been at that crossroad in my town at the same moment as Don Segundo?

Luck, luck! There's nothing to do but face you squarely, and accept you, fair or foul, as you happen to come.

It's a good thing for the herder that he lives too

close to life to be able to lose himself in speculations that might make a coward of him. The imperious daily tasks leave him no time to brood over his defeats; either he plays the game or he gives up when he's lost the will to stand up to life. Let him go soft because of a momentary anguish and he runs the risk of drinking the same bitter brew as any animal that admits defeat: death. Every moment of his life calls for faith, and only from himself can he draw it, for the weak, the pampa is a blind alley. Law of the strong: either hang on to what is yours or go for good.

What except complete self-confidence made my godfather so cool in the worst emergency? I think he never got upset because he was always prepared for the worst and could meet any problem with a smile. "I can't fall any farther than the ground," says the wrangler to the men who predict that he's going to be thrown. There's a limit to everything, he means; and when all is said and done, strength is simply not to be afraid. "Death won't pass me up," my godfather seemed to say, "and when it comes, it won't scare me and I'll be ready."

The result was that while everyone was heading toward death, he seemed to be on the way back. Suffering, I saw more than once, was to him like his daily bread, and he never complained unless a bruise or wound kept him from moving. "The carcass," as he called his body, "has no right to say no, when you give it a job." However, all these thoughts of mine were mere conjecture. The only thing I was sure of was his indifference to events, which he faced with ironic understanding.

Oh, to be like him! I who was at the mercy of everything, like water affected by the lay of the land, the wind, the sun, the weeping willow leaf that drops upon its surface. And there were always worries in my head, buzzing and creeping into every corner of my mind.

But to get back to events: we rode around for a week without finding work. Then we were taken on as helpers in a drive of six hundred yearlings that a rancher was sending to pasture. That meant, according to those who knew, about twelve days on the road, if the weather held and the condition of the herd stayed good. The afternoon we started was hot and sultry; just saddling made us sweat, and every creature, every blade of grass, was waiting for one of those storms that flatten one out with their fury and then set you straight again, like sprouting grass. Even before we started, we were drenched by a couple of slanting squalls that packed the soft dirt of the corrals and roads like a rash. But the body of the storm was still overhead, waiting for us in a great pile of black clouds to the south. As it might turn very chilly afterward, we prepared for a hard march.

We had already had supper and it was dark when, after a moment of sultry heat, a stiff wind sprang up. Lightning for some time had been streaking the black clouds on the southern horizon. The herd was nervous, and getting worse. The horses neighed uneasily, feeling, as we did, the tension in the air. It was a perfect night for losing animals! Every flash revealed, livid, the imperturbable countryside and our uneasy herd moving about it, hemmed in by the herders. An ominous, formless something was going to fall upon us from above at any minute. Things stood out in the flickering light with uncanny clearness; and the white steers and the silvery roan and the spotted ones seemed to fill the eye. The next instant we were lost in the black night, the swift vision branded on our minds like scars on hide, and we groped ahead until another flash. After the wind came a hush. In the sky were great ponds and silvery rivers against a background of flat black pools. And yet tatters of gray cloud scurried across it in wild confusion, like mustangs flying before a prairie fire.

The overseer warned us to keep a close watch on the steers who were milling around, lost in their own fear. A bolt of lightning struck the earth with a dry crack that seemed to split our flesh. The wind, it seemed to me, was coming from underground. The herd split up like a lump of limestone in water. We remembered that we had to cross the bed of a deep gulch, and we galloped hard to forestall the threat of beasts falling, breaking their legs and getting mired down in the bottom. I could not see a thing. The ends of my neckerchief flew in my face, my hat brim flapped in my eyes; the wind kept me from guiding my horse, but he ran on, perhaps because he could not stop and had lost his bearings like the cattle.

I sensed a dark mass running ahead of me: probably a horse that had broken loose from some carriage overpowered by the wind. Men, women? Whoever they were, God help them. I dashed ahead until I was abreast of a bunch of steers. By now the rain was coming down in torrents and the wind was letting up. I heard one of the men yell and I set out in the direction of his shout. The two of us fought together to keep the steers, pushing each other, from going over the side of the gulch. My horse's hind feet slipped and I went down, down like hell had swallowed me, without knowing where. By luck the slide stopped before my horse rolled over on me. As he reared up on his haunches I could see that he was trampling a calf. I could not hold him. Terror was riding him, and he fell on his right side, pinning my leg for a moment against a big clod in the gully. Then, laboriously, he got to his feet, slipped, and fell again on his haunches. Again and again. At last, his body tense with will, he gave a mighty upward lurch and we made it.

Meanwhile, the storm had passed like a hawk over a chicken yard. Dimly we made each other out and set to work to round up the scattered yearlings. I told the overseer what had happened to me in the bottom of the gulch. If my horse had trampled one steer, there was reason to believe there were others there, who had fallen and couldn't get out. We all went down to search, except those who were riding herd. With our ropes and even with our hands, we toiled to get the fallen on their feet and slaughter those that couldn't. Our horses floundered about in the churned mud and more than once lost their footing. We had to be ready to slide free if our ponies fell, for the least carelessness might cost us a

fractured bone, cracking with the sound of a sliver of
wood. When at last we came up, plastered to the eyes
with mud, we had to leave five steers dying in the dark
hole. As we set out we sent a messenger ahead to the
next town to find a butcher and sell him the disabled
animals at his own price. And the same messenger was
to send a man back to tell the owner what had happened. As the ranch was near town, he'd know soon
enough.

The storm had left the animals so nervous that we
had to ride around them by fours. The night continued
sultry and stifling. The cloudburst with its lightning and
its whirling winds had done us little good.

By the light of a yellowish dawn we followed the trail
after the overseer had counted the steaming beasts. All
that day we stopped only to eat our three meals. The
bad start had depressed us, and as the animals were
still rebellious, we kept them traveling to wear them
down and quiet them. And then night, and we were riding herd on them.

I had, in addition to the general ones, troubles of my
own. I had only three good ponies: Moro, Vinchuca,
Guasquita, the survivors of my old string, and the two
colts I had won in payment for breaking the bays. I
could not count on the tricky bay, and the other, until
he was through his apprenticeship, was a gamble.

The third day dealt us another pleasant surprise. We
were crossing an open stretch of country, with the sun
still low in the northeast, when suddenly the herd scattered. We had a bunch of some thirty young bulls who
were born troublemakers; they would start a fight on
the least provocation and acted, most of the time, like
rowdies at a celebration. A red and white was the worst
and several times already he had locked horns with a
white one till we beat them apart with the butts of our
quirts. He didn't know the meaning of obedience, and
when he got hot there was no stopping him.

The herd's scattering was taffy for the two young
braves, and they went at it hot and heavy. We closed in
on them like flies. By bad luck a fellow named Demetrio

happened to pass the red and white just as he had got
his foe's neck down and was putting all his strength into
a lunge. The white, squirming like a snake, turned his
flank; the other, overreaching, struck Demetrio's horse.
Although the young bull had only a piece of thick,
broken horn on his right side, he drove it deep in the
horse's flank, tearing out his guts. While three of us
roped the raging animal and dragged him off, the rest of
us fell on his victim like vultures; the owner had to cut
his throat—and I bid for the hide for boots, the others
bid for straps, and in the time it takes to say Amen we
had the poor devil skinned and sold.

All that night we kept to the trail, but we had the
bad luck to run into two other herds and had to stand
watch for the third time!

We were really getting tired out! And my troubles
were not those of a tenderfoot. I knew that if you can
stand a lot because your body has grown hardened, you
stand a lot more because you've taught your will not to
give in. The body suffers only at first; then it grows numb
and goes without resisting wherever you take it. Later
your thoughts begin to grow cloudy; you don't know how
near you are to the goal, you don't know if you will ever
reach it. Later still, thoughts and facts get mixed into
something so unreal that you become indifferent and
watch it dimly moving beyond your ken. Finally all that
is left is the strength to go on without flinching, to go
on forever. For this, and by this, you live, all else has
vanished except your unbreakable will. And at the end
you win (at least so it had been with me) after winning
itself has become a matter of indifference. Your body
falls asleep only because your will has left it.

Six days more we moved through cold and drench-
ings, standing watch every night, always on the alert,
crossing swamps and mudflats, piling one layer of fatigue
on another. My reserve horse gave me a hard day's
work; at the slightest chance, when I was driving or roping, he was up to his tricks. So I gave him the quirt,
thong and handle, without stopping, till I had him tamed.

Maybe I would kill him? It was no time for standing on ceremony.

We looked like a band of pampa Indians, ragged, muddied, sullen. Demetrio, the biggest and strongest of the herders, seemed overcome by fatigue. And which of us would take oath that he was in better shape? At last we came to a place that promised a rest. There was a small enclosed pasture where the herd could be left without risk, and for us, a shed where we could sleep under a roof! We got there early in the afternoon, drove in the herd, and rode our horses slowly toward the shed. Demetrio was riding ahead. When he reached the hitching post, his horse shied. Demetrio fell like a sack of maté and lay without moving. He had struck his head. Had the sudden terrible fall broken his neck? We rushed up. He was breathing like a child.

Don Segundo laughed. "He was a little tired—the fall rocked him to sleep."

We unsaddled his horse, stretched his outfit in the shade, and laid him on it. He lay, unaware of how sleep had tricked him, but perhaps he was feeling the bliss of letting his body go, of wanting nothing in the world.

The rest of us sat around for a while drinking maté. We had the assurance of a quiet night ahead and this made us happy and talkative. We watered our ponies, rubbed them down. We looked over our outfits, mending a strap, sewing a pair of hobbles, adjusting a saddle or a halter. We waited calmly for the night to come closer little by little, something great and gentle upon which we could softly float away as on a river between whose banks flows the joy of ease and forgetfulness.

25

It was a little late when we got up; the sun was rising. Demetrio had slept twelve hours and we eight. It was enough to take the numbness out of us, although our bodies still complained; we were ready, after a couple of matés, for another day. The trouble I had foreseen had grown worse. My three good horses were worn out, the tough bay was half dead from our battles, and the other colt was none too frisky. What to do? It would be shameful to ask the overseer for my pay and drop out. My godfather might lend me a horse or two from his own string, but that would leave him where I was now.

Thick in gloom I was, and the sun already high when we came to the outskirts of Navarro. Strange! This place, which now saw me broke and crestfallen, had witnessed my greatest joy and pride! Right through here I had ridden, sidewise on my Weasel, who knew how to pace, bubbling over with self-love and stroking the good luck that fattened my belt—the ten-peso bills of the

cockfight. What a day that had been! What a gamecock
the red, with his cracked beak, fighting without giving
up for a whole hour, waiting for his chance and knowing how to take it when it came! I laughed when I
thought of my nerve, taking and laying all those bets,
just because I believed in myself. And that cocksure ar-
rogance of a spoiled kid with which I had pocketed the
winnings. Sure, I had thought then, this is my destiny:
to sit forever on the top of the world! And the lunch at
the hotel, the noisy chattering gringos, the Spaniard who
talked of pilgrimages . . .

One memory, naturally enough, brings on another. But
for a memory to bring on a man . . . that's not so common! Someone was riding next to my godfather, and I
don't know why, I felt they were talking of me. It was
someone I knew—knew well. Of course! It was Pedro
Barrales! Why did I not feel as happy as I should? I
trotted over, just the same, despite my strange mood, to
greet my old friend. And was amazed to see him touch
his hat to me, to hear his formal "How are you?"

"What's the matter, brother?" I said, hurt and confused. "If you've got something against me, out with it!
But don't go pouting like a woman."

Pedro turned confused and inquiringly to my godfather.

Don Segundo spoke up, "To begin with, hold your
horses and don't run wild, for you'll be needing a cool
head. Pedro has some news for you. Here's a paper that
will give it to you straighter than a lot of talk. Thank
God, you're no woman, and you've not been brought
up so delicate that a shock will kill you. Here, now you're
prepared, take it."

The envelope read: Señor Fabio Cáceres.

"What's this got to do with me?" I almost shouted.

"Open it," said my godfather.

The letter was signed by Don Leandro Galván, and
it read:

Dear young friend,
*   I don't doubt that the contents of this note will*

come as a surprise to you. I am afraid the shock may be rather sudden, but the truth is I have no other way of communicating with you.

Your father, Fabio Cáceres, is dead, and has left . . .

All of a sudden I saw many things: my trips to the ranch, my ponies, my aunts—then they really were my aunts! I looked around. Pedro and my godfather had moved on ahead. So had the herd. A strange loneliness gripped my heart, as if it had suddenly been shut in a cell, a small cell. I got off my horse, leaned against a wire fence, and went on reading:

Your father, Fabio Cáceres, is dead and has left to me the difficult, thankless duty of carrying out what he always intended to do. . . .

I skipped a few lines:

so I am your guardian until you come of age.

I got back on my horse. The country, everything, was changed. I was looking at the world from inside somebody else! A herd of feelings, unknown to me before, milled in my head: tenderness, sadness. And suddenly blind rage, as if I had been humiliatingly and wantonly insulted. The devil! I had to lash out at someone, anything. There had to be body blood drawn for this soul blood I felt bubbling within me.

I caught up with Don Segundo and Pedro. My godfather said that, since it was impossible, things being as they were, for me to go on with the herd, I had better arrange with the overseer to get myself replaced.

"And you?" I broke in.

"I am going with you," he answered quietly.

Feeling this affection so near me turned my rage to pain. I realized that I was a child, an orphan, and I was losing, at a blow, something I had lived by, had clung to. I turned to my godfather. "For God's sake, Don

Segundo, tell me this paper is a joke. I'm nobody's son and I don't have to receive advice or money or even a name from anyone." I had a momentary vision of Don Fabio. "This dead father of mine, what was he like, playing around so fast and loose with the ranch girls!"

"Slow, boy," my godfather interrupted. "Slow! Your father did not run after the girls, and he was not shameless. Your father was a rich man like all the other rich men and no worse than any of them. That's all I've got to say to you, except that you've got a lot to learn, and some day, without anyone's help, you'll learn that what I say is the truth."

"And my mother?"

"A saint like my own."

I asked no more; what he had said was enough to make me believe that my mother had been worthy of all respect. As for my father, the one bad thing about *him* was that he was rich! What evil was that? Did my godfather mean that I would learn that evil soon enough from my own experience—from being rich myself? Was there scorn in his prophecy?

Pretty soon I got myself in hand. I had been acting like a child and had better keep quiet. But what hurt most was that Pedro already looked on me as a stranger. When I recalled how politely he had addressed me, it made me so mad that I lost my head again.

"As for you," I said, pulling my horse alongside his, "all you can do, now, I reckon, is to say sir to me, and touch your hat, seeing I've got a few pesos and can help you or harm you with my money."

Pedro turned pale at the insult and raised his quirt to bring the handle down on my head. To die of a knife cut on the trail? Was that my destiny? So be it! Anything was better than false respect and estrangement from my friends.

"Come on down," I said softly, slipping off my pony with my knife in my hand. But my godfather was standing in front of me and took me by the arm.

"If you've fallen off your horse, I'll help you back up."

I understood that if I disobeyed I'd get a beating. And

that made me happy in a way others might not understand. To Don Segundo I was still the orphan brat. And to show how grateful I was, I gave him a name I had never before thought of using: "All right, Dad."

"If I'm your dad, you'll ask this man's pardon for insulting him."

"Brother"—and I held out my hand—"will you forgive me?"

Pedro laughed, as if to show he was beaten, and said heartily, "One can see you grew up wild!"

Thus the first troubles of my new life were settled, and I decided to keep my mouth shut, so that I could think. Think? And how could I master the horde of notions that swarmed into my brain, and as fast as they came were crowded out by others even wilder? I could find neither reason nor words. All I got for my pains were images that followed one another with helter-skelter swiftness. I saw myself face to face with Don Leandro, haughtily refusing my inheritance. "If the dead man would not acknowledge me as his son while he was alive, I refuse to acknowledge him as my father now he is dead." I saw myself on the estate, dictating to a lawyer my plans for cutting up the land and parceling it among the poor. I imagined myself fleeing from my respectability as Martin Fierro fled from the posse. . . . Oh, hell! How to get order from this chaos?

At last, thank God, I wore myself out. My eyes dropped to my horse's mane. From the mane they passed to the placid neck as he went trotting monotonously along. From the neck to the ears, alert to some noise; behind his ears, my look traveled to the headband of his bridle and my clothes. My silver-studded belt was the one bright thing about me. How shabby and worn with work were my blouse and breeches! Must I throw all this away?

It is hard to believe, but instead of rejoicing over the riches fate had dropped in my hands, I grieved for the poverty I was losing. Why? Because behind this lay all my days as a wandering herder, and deeper still, that vague need to be forever on the move, which is like a thirst for the road and a longing, which grew each day, to possess the round earth!

At my request we went over where the herd was and I took leave of my companions. With each handshake I felt that I was saying good-bye to myself. And when I got to the last one, it seemed the end of me. Finally, we turned our backs on the riders. All the pains I had suffered to make myself a capable herder stayed in my mind like the heaped-up bones of a dead man.

We spent the night at the same ranch, with the same man who had taken us in after the cockfight. Everything was cordial except my silence. As the day dimmed, moment by moment I felt myself slipping away; it was as though a series of links, joining me to my world, were painfully breaking. I felt myself removed even from the talk of the three men.

Something I could not understand weighed down my mind.

My sleep was a procession of nightmares and of thoughts that revolved around the same idea: my arrival at Don Leandro's, the refusal of my ill-gotten inheritance, my flight. My weary mind kept harping on that same theme till I was dazed but saw no way to escape. By morning I was as limp as a wet quirt. I got up to end my sufferings and went out to saddle my horse with the sensation that I was leaving my soul behind me on the pampas.

Don Segundo and Pedro were saddling too. We went through the same motions, and yet how different we were! Different? And why? Suddenly, in the comparison, I had found the source of my unhappiness: *I was no longer a gaucho!* The thought stunned me. I had put my suffering into words and with these words I was lashed to the heart of my sorrow. I finished the saddling. The sun rose. We went to the kitchen for some bitter matés. Nothing of all this mattered any more.

Silently we had been taking turns at the *bombilla,* sipping one by one, when I said, half to myself: "Now, I suppose, we'll gallop over to Don Leandro's place. People will talk to me there as if I were newborn. Then they'll hand over the property and the pesos. Is that it?"

Without knowing what I was driving at, Pedro nodded. "That's it."

"Later I'll take charge of the whole establishment; I'll chuck these rags and dress like a gentleman. I'll begin to give orders and be served like a magnate. Is that it?"

"Uh-huh."

"And that means I'll no longer be a gaucho?"

My godfather watched me steadily. For the first time he seemed really surprised, or perhaps merely curious. "What difference does that make?" he asked.

"Of course! What difference does it make? Well, I'll tell you. I'd rather the vultures had picked my flesh to shreds, I'd rather have left my bones, like a wild animal's beside some water hole, I'd rather lose myself on the pampa like an outlaw! Rather than all these nice things fate has blessed me with today, I would have preferred to die by the law in which I was raised and lived, for I'm not a snake to be shedding my skin or bettering my appearance!"

Don Segundo got up, a sign that it was time to start. I took his arm anxiously and asked, "Is it true I'm not what I was and that these God-damned pesos will wipe out my gaucho life?"

"Look," said my godfather, and laying a hand on my shoulder and smiling, "if you're a true gaucho, you won't change, for wherever you go your soul will go before you, leading you like a bell mare."

26

The mares and the old horses knew they were on the way home. I too felt the approach to my home town, which I had left so frustrated and unhappy, vowing I would never return. The place we come from is a little fatherland, and however far away we go shreds of it, gathered in joy and sorrow, remain in us and with time become flesh of our flesh. Without riding too hard that night we reached Luján. Next morning we set out again, and my eyes began to discover familiar objects, as in a deliberately recalled dream. The special smell of the fields and of some brook entered my heart as though it were their home.

We spent the night at La Blanqueada. What memories! The owner slapped me on the back and made me welcome. At last, he said, "Well, son, now I'm at your orders. Take whatever you like, and pay me cash on the barrel head, the way you made me pay for your catfish."

I liked that! If only all of them would receive me in

this fashion! Or would they show me a false and dis-
gusting deference? I slept well that night in the patio at
La Blanqueada.

We weren't due at Don Leandro's until afternoon, so
I had a chance to learn people's real intentions by the
way they treated me. The barber greeted me as though I
were one of those princes in fairy tales. He wore himself out, calling me "Señor" and "Don"; and he seemed
to remember nothing about my former poverty, nor my
present attire nor the small tips that he used to hand me
in the old days for doing some odd job. The jeweler
opened his showcases when he saw me coming; neither
could he remember the time he just missed me with a
broom—that day a gang of us kids had asked him if the
silver he used in his work was strong enough to stand by
itself or still needed the help of friends. The bigwigs of
the town whom I used to entertain with my pranks were
more affectionate than they used to be, and from the way
some of them looked at me I could tell that they were
seeing a halo of gold coins around my head.

I swore that barber would never cut my hair, nor that
jeweler sell me a buckle, nor the bigwigs pay for my
drinks. Anyway, years ago, I had crossed them off my
list, and the cross was still there. At noon we ate with
Don Segundo at La Blanqueada and there were as many
jokes and memories and plans as there was food. Don
Pedro sure was a gaucho of a saloonkeeper! He asked
me a thousand questions, not about my money, but about
the years I had been away, wanting to know if I could
really ride, and how I was with the rope, and how many
steps of the *malambo* I had learned, and could I skin a
horse to make a pair of boots? While we talked, he
casually lifted an embroidered tobacco pouch from the
pocket of my blouse, and when the meal was over, he
went out to wait on his customers with no more ceremony than an "Excuse me," seeing he had no helper.

A little later we were on the road again, headed for
Galván's place. As we drew near, I thought of my
clothes. I had not changed a single garment, and what I
wanted was a new *chiripá*, new shoes, shirt, and necker-

chief, so as to be well dressed but still a gaucho. The good hours with Don Pedro began to fade away, and once more I began to worry about my situation.

Before, true enough, I had been nothing but a gaucho, but now I was a bastard son who had been hidden away for a long time as something disgraceful. In my former situation I did not have to think about my birth: orphan and gaucho were one, for, as I saw it, both meant child of God, child of the pampas, child of oneself! Even to be a legitimate son, the fact of bearing a name that implied family and rank would have seemed to me a lessening of my freedom; something like changing from a cloud into a tree that is the slave of its roots and tied to a few square feet of ground. The thought came to me that I was going to have a talk with a rich man and that I was what rich folk called a "family dishonor."

To hell with it all!

We got down at the hitching rail of the farmhands and went into the kitchen. Nobody was there. A boy came in and said the boss was waiting for me in the patio under the bead trees. I knew the way and there I found Don Leandro just like the time when I had brewed him his maté.

"Come over, friend," he said when he saw me. I took off my hat, and walked toward him, and took the hand he was holding out. But he looked at me with an affection that upset me.

"How big you are and grown up!" he said. "Don't be ashamed. You knew me as boss, but now I'm your guardian, and that is almost like a father when the guardian is what he should be. You're tired, I see," he went on, pretending that was the reason for my pallor. "I'll not bother you now with details nor with advice. There's plenty of time ahead for that, God willing."

I seemed to have stopped hearing him. His voice went on: ". . . you've seen the world, now, my lad, and you've become a man—better than a man, a gaucho. The one who knows the world's evils because he has lived through them is tempered to overcome them."

What were these words that I had heard already? I

had lived all that in a world of dreams. Near us there was a rosebush in bloom and a spotted dog sniffed at my boots. I had my hat in my hand and I was happy—happy and sad. Why? Strange things had happened to me, making me almost someone else—someone who had achieved a great thing, but at the price of death!

"Stay here as long as you like," the voice was droning on. "Your ranch is waiting for you, and I'm here, when you need me. . . ."

This seemed to end the talk, and Don Leandro called out toward the hands' kitchen, "Raucho!"

I felt good in spite of the moral crisis I had suffered. I had a strange feeling of a new existence.

A big boy, dressed in gaucho fashion, came out and stopped beside me.

"Take this lad," Don Leandro ordered, "to turn his horse into the corral, show him his room, help him if he needs anything; let's see if you get to be friends."

"All right, Father."

As we walked toward the hitching rail, I looked at my future friend. He was bigger than I, though he did not seem older. Ranch life was stamped all over him, and he gave me the impression of strength, self-confidence, and gay good humor. He was handsome, too, with fine features and a frank, intelligent expression. All in all a regular gaucho!

"You're the son of the boss?" I couldn't help asking.

He smiled. "So they say—and so he says."

We reached the post, and he jumped on a newly broken roan colt. Again, I asked, "Do you break your own ponies?"

"I did, until you came." He used the familiar *tu* at once, like a good scout. I looked again at his agreeable face, his clothes, his saddle outfit.

"What are you staring at?" it was his turn to ask.

I wanted to give him back some of his own good-natured banter, so I said, "D'you know what you are?"

"Let's hear."

"You're a dude gaucho."

"The pot calling the kettle black!" He laughed. "I'm

a dude gaucho, and pretty soon you'll be a gaucho dude."

And we both laughed.

He showed me his string of ponies, and we went back to the house, having unsaddled and turned the horses out to pasture. He took me to what was to be my room. Then I looked up at Raucho.

"Don't feel at home here?" he asked.

"I think I'll spend the whole night admiring the little flowers on the wallpaper!" I talked to him frankly, like a brother, something I couldn't have done with any other rich person.

And he answered, "Look here. If you want to spread your saddle blankets in the barn and sleep there, I will too."

"Great!"

Raucho got permission to eat in the kitchen with the men. And Don Leandro must have understood my shyness and told his son to keep me company. We had a round of matés with Don Segundo and Valerio, who was very glad to see me. My memories moved me, and as Raucho with his ways and clothes made me forget the change in my fortunes, I took him along wherever I could best recall the past.

"Here's where I slept the first night! I swept out these sheep pens before sunup. Is the pony Frog still alive? Oh, boy, you should have seen how happy I was when I came back from the Cuevas place with that dun! Does Cuevas still live there?"

I waited breathless for an answer. My mouth was dry.

"No. They've not been there for a long time."

We spent most of that night talking, my new friend and I. I don't ever remember talking so much. And it seemed the first time I had ever really thought of the events of my life. Until then there had been no time! How can a man look back and evaluate the past when the present keeps him forever on the alert? A lot you can meditate when every second you've got to deal with life itself! Just let your wits go wandering when there's a skittish colt between your legs; just try to cast up your griefs and joys when the health of your skin and success depend on how sharp your attention is! To be sure, I had thought plenty, but always from the viewpoint of the present. I had thought the way a man thinks when he is in a fight, with his eyes keyed to danger and all his strength on tap to be brought into play without a moment's delay. This sorting out of images from the past was something very different. I had lived in an eternal morning full of the will to reach its noon, but now it was like an afternoon, and I let myself sink into myself and found peace in the contemplation of what had been.

Like a brook that flows into a quiet pool I kept going around in circles; I felt deep, full of profound stillness. At last I tired of talking and searching my soul. I remained quiet for a long time.

My friend was already asleep. So much the better! There was the night, and I its image.

To die for a while—

Until the rays of dawn slit my eyes open.

27

The lagoon raised frothy ripples against the bank, and in the center, among sparse reeds, wild birds were screeching. My body and my thoughts were loaded down with a great weariness, as if I were surfeited with going through the world forever sowing useless deeds.

A bitter moment lay ahead of me, the moment that, more than any other in my life, meant a severing. It was three years since I had left off being a simple herder and had come into my domain. . . . My domain! I could look around, all around, and say to myself, "This is mine!" But the words meant nothing. When, in gaucho days, had I ever felt that I was riding through the fields of someone else? And who owns the pampa if not the gaucho? It made me smile to think of all the "owners" of ranches, shut up tight in their houses, fretted by cold and heat, and scared of the least danger of a bucking horse, a wild bull, a windstorm. Owners of what? A patch of land on a survey map marked with their name, but all God's pampa had been mine, for I had won it by my strength and my skill!

It is clear that in my life water is a mirror that reflects the images of what has been. At the edge of a brook, long ago, I had gone over my childhood. At the ford of a river where I was watering my pony, I had looked back on my five years of apprenticeship as a gaucho. And now, on the bank of a lagoon on my own land, I mentally consulted my diary as an owner.

If I had done as I wished when I received my ranch from Don Leandro, I should still be leaving the hoofprints of my string of ponies on lands forever new. Two reasons had changed my mind at the time: the advice of my guardian, which seemed sound, and the corroboration of his counsels by my godfather. But the clinching argument was Don Segundo's promise to stay with me!

For the first two years I was really living on *his* ranch! I scarcely looked at the main house; my wild instincts were too alive. I spread my blankets outdoors and shunned all confinement. I got up, like any gaucho, with the dawn and went to sleep with the chickens.

The big bare house, filled with furniture as gloomy as my aunts, only got glimpses of me. Its cavernous rooms still belonged to that man whom I could not bring myself to think of as my father. Besides, the house seemed to be dying; its presence but a chill memory. If I had dared, I'd have torn it down as you cut the throat of a suffering beast out of pity.

The colt lot, over which Don Segundo reigned, was next to Galván's place, and so we often got together with Raucho. Our friendship had been speedily sealed, and as proof of it, we exchanged ponies. He gave me the first gallops of some bays, fulfilling my old dream of a string of that color, and I returned the gift with the same number of sorrels. We helped each other in the breaking. It was a true gaucho friendship. For two boys who were in the saddle from sunup to sundown it was a way of being in one another's thoughts all the time.

Aside from the time Don Leandro had us over at his study teaching us the ins and outs of running a ranch, we spent all the time we could with Don Segundo. And those hours with my godfather were the best of all; with the maté passing from hand to hand or strumming a guitar, while the grand old man told stories, tales or adventures of his own life, with that clarity and grace that I have tried to evoke in these recollections!

One result of our talks was that Raucho won me over to some of his own hobbies. He knew a lot about reading and books, and he loaned me a few and discussed them at length with me. But what a difference between us! I had a hard time reading even my own language, while he was as much at home in French, Italian, English as in Spanish! Just the same, he often seemed a child to me, a child unbaptized by the waters of life and innocent of suffering. Another topic of conversation was his love affairs and amusements. What was he after? Life as it was, it seemed to me, was full enough, and to try to twist it into novel combinations seemed to me pathetically childish. But my simple arguments made no dent on his fantastic notions; so at last I let him talk himself out to his heart's content. Moreover, the circumstances of my own birth made it impossible for me to look on a love affair as sport.

Little by little my new character and my new tastes were being formed. Along with my everyday occupations, I began to feel the need to express myself in words. And then I set myself to study in dead earnest. . . .

But it is not of that I want to speak in these simple pages. Suffice it to say that the lessons of Don Leandro, the books, a few visits with Raucho to Buenos Aires, were gradually making me over into what is called an educated man. Yet for joy and deep satisfaction, nothing took the place of my rustic life. Although I did not turn my back on the new ways of living and took a somewhat dour pleasure in my intellectual training, something untamed and hostile remained with me from the past.

And that afternoon I was to suffer the severest blow of all.

I looked at my watch. It was five o'clock. I got on my horse and trotted toward the road where I was to meet my godfather. It was impossible to hold him back any longer. I had begged, I had insisted. But he was born to go, always to go—and three years in one place was all the immobility he could endure! The pull of every trail was too strong in myself for me not to understand how, for Don Segundo, life and the road were one. To think that I had to stay!

We greeted each other the same as always.

We trotted along, side by side, for a few miles down the road. We made a shortcut through a meadow to save time and came to a hill called "The White Bull" where we had agreed to say good-bye. We had not spoken. What for?

His rough hand, pressing mine, imposed silence upon me. Sadness is cowardice. Once again, with a smile, we wished each other luck. Don Segundo's horse turned away from mine, and in that divergence of our paths I felt all that was to separate our destinies.

I watched him ride away. My eyes rested on his familiar motions. For an instant, I did not know if I was seeing . . . or remembering. I knew how he would raise his quirt, opening his hand a little, and how his body would lean forward as the horse broke into a gallop. So it was. The change of pace, from trot to gallop, shook his body like laughter. Then the familiar measure of the hoofs threshing distance. To gallop is to abolish distance, and to arrive, for the gaucho, is but a pretext for leaving.

Down the trail, which seemed a rivulet of dirt, horse and rider reached the brow of the hill, merged with the thistles. For a moment the double silhouette stood in bright profile against the sky crossed slantwise by a greenish ray of the sun. An idea—not a man—was disappearing. Suddenly it was gone, and my meditation was cut off from its source.

I said to myself, "Now, he is going past the canebrake. After he has crossed the stream, I'll see him appear over the second hill." Night was conquering day—slowly, surely, as one who has no fear of the outcome. Thin clouds held filaments of light.

The shrunken silhouette of my godfather appeared on

the hillside. It seemed to me too soon. Yet it was he,
I felt sure of it; despite the distance, he was not far
away. My gaze clung to that tiny movement on the som-
nolent pampa. Soon he would reach the crest of the
trail and disappear. He grew smaller, as if he were being
whittled away from below. My eyes held fast to the black
spot of his hat, to make the last trace of him endure.
It was useless. My sight grew blurred—perhaps it was
the effort I was making—and a light of tiny vibrancies
spread over the pampa. I do not know what strange

suggestion made me feel the limitless presence of a
soul.

"*Sombra* . . . shadow," I murmured to myself. And I
began to think, almost violently, of my adopted father.
Pray? Simply let my sorrow flow? I do not know all
the things that crowded into my loneliness. But they were
thoughts a man never confesses to himself.

I concentrated my will on doing the little trivial things,

turned my horse about, and slowly set out toward the ranch.

I went like one whose lifeblood is flowing away.

La Portena
March, 1926

Glossary

ALPARGATAS—canvas sandals with rope soles.

BOLAS—gaucho weapon consisting of three stones, each sewed in a leather casing and joined by a plaited leather rope. The two larger stones are at the ends, the smaller one in the center. The gaucho whirls the bolas about his head and lets it fly at the feet of the ostrich, of the enemy's horse, of any animal he wants to catch; the stones entangle the legs and bring the animal down.

BOMBILLA—sipper through which the herb maté is drunk from a gourd. It is made of metal, often of silver.

CABURÉ—small bird of the owl family.

CHAJÁ—a small bird that, when startled, utters a cry similar in sound to its name.

CHINITA—literally "little China girl"; Argentine country girl, usually but not necessarily part Indian.

CAUDILLO—chieftain or leader of a small band of fighters who usually recognize no law but his word.

CHIRIPÁ—long, fringed shawl worn by the gaucho, held at the waist by a belt.

GATO—country dance, rapid in movement, with much heel
   work and tapping.

GUACHO—orphan, waif, foundling.

MALAMBO—country dance of slow sensuous rhythm.

MANDINGA—the devil. The term is probably of Indian
   origin.

MATÉ—the classic drink of Argentina. It is the leaf of
   an herb grown in tropical (Northern) Argentina,
   and Paraguay and Brazil; it is brewed like tea. It is
   drunk in a small gourd (called also the maté) and
   with the *bombilla*. It is so rich in vitamins and salts
   that, with meat, it makes a perfect diet for the
   gaucho, who scarcely knows fresh vegetables.

OMBÚ—a thick, wide-spreading elephantine tree, greatly
   celebrated in Argentine song and story. It is said
   to be the one tree native to the pampas.

PRADO—country dance.

QUEBRACHO—literally "ax-breaker"; a tree of northerly
   Argentina whose wood resembles mahogany and is
   so hard and resilient that it is almost impossible to
   cut it.

RETARJO—opprobrious epithet.

TABA—knucklebone of the sheep, used like dice in a
   game of the same name. It is marked merely
   "heads" and "tails."

TERO—a nocturnal bird of the pampas.

TRIUNFO—country dance.

Afterword

The perceptive reader, when he has finished *Don Segundo Sombra,* will realize that for all its panoply of detailed description and local color, its uniquely Argentine flavor, he has been reading, in the first instance, a fairy tale. It is a version of the Cinderella story, of the dispossessed heir who finally comes into his patrimony, of the youth who, under the guidance of a tutelary spirit—Don Segundo— overcomes the trials he must undergo to prove himself worthy of the rewards in store for him. Or if fairy tale seems a little fanciful, we can replace it by myth, a term which enjoys greater prestige. In *Don Segundo Sombra* Güiraldes has distilled the essence of the pampa and the gaucho, the two cornerstones of Argentine mythology.

Before Güiraldes two other writers had produced works which are classics of Argentine—and Hispanic— literature and which deal with this same material: Domingo F. Sarmiento in his *Facundo, or Civilization and Barbarism in the Argentine Republic* (1845) and José Hernández with his magnificent epic poem *Martín*

Fierro (1872). When the forces of the dictator Juan Manuel Rosas triumphed in Sarmiento's native province of San Juan and he miraculously escaped the death sentence passed on him, he emigrated to Chile. *Facundo* was his answer to Rosas's demand that the Chilean government put a stop to the activities of the Argentine exiles, especially the "savage, perfidious, traitorous Sarmiento." Instead of directly attacking Rosas, who in his eyes represented all that was retrograde and stood in the way of Argentina's becoming the great nation Sarmiento envisaged (and which it became, in large measure, under his presidency), he incarnated everything that Rosas stood for in the figure of Facundo Quiroga, one of his gaucho generals who, when he threatened to become a rival, was assassinated, probably at Rosas's orders. Yet Sarmiento could never have left us this unforgettable picture of the gaucho with all his shortcomings—and his virtues— if he had not understood Quiroga, "The Tiger of the Plains," as one understands only that which one carries within oneself. Proof of the fact that Sarmiento was aware of this was his remark that one had only to look under the frock coat of an Argentine to find the gaucho.

The originality of *Martín Fierro*—and in this it resembles other great works of Hispanic literature—consists in its lack of originality, in the fact that everything it says had been said before, but never so completely or so well. Its themes and metrical pattern had been established in the anonymous folk poetry of the river Plate region by the *payadores,* or bards: the gaucho's protest against the hateful laws promulgated in Buenos Aires, the enforced military service, the curtailment of his liberty. The reason for the book's immediate and enduring popularity was that every word in it aroused a familiar echo in its readers or hearers, for it came to be recited like authentic folk poetry. The language, the simple, sententious philosophy, the humor, the wisdom were all typically, authentically those of the gaucho, but expressed with an ease and mastery that were beyond him. This was Hernández's rare achievement: that he, an educated man of the city (though he had spent his youth on the family ranch), was able to think and express himself as only a gaucho could have done. In *Facundo* we see the gaucho at his zenith; in *Martín Fierro* he is already doomed to disappearance, with the arrival of ever-increasing numbers of European immigrants, the growing power of Buenos Aires, the fencing off of his once limitless domains, and his melancholy submergence in the rising tide of civilization. In *Don Segundo Sombra* he has become a memory, and an act of piety and faith.

Perhaps there never was a gaucho quite like Don Segundo, so "compleat and parfait," but this is of no consequence. In spite of the fact that the reader lives the life of the pampa, endures its heat and its dust, shares in the work and excitement of the drives and roundups, the brandings, the horse breaking, this is not a realistic work. Like William Henry Hudson—whom, to the slightly annoyed surprise of the English-speaking world, the Argentines claim as their own—Güiraldes has captured the poetic truth, the eternal quality of the scenes and personages he describes, which is the highest form of reality. As Pablo Rojas Paz, a gifted writer and friend of Güiraldes, says: "Sarmiento is descriptive, Hernández narrative, Güiraldes poetic. Sarmiento needs persons, Hernández facts, for Güiraldes, evocation suffices."

Ricardo Güiraldes (1886–1927) came of an old family of the landowning aristocracy of Argentina. His boyhood was spent between the family's city home in Buenos Aires and the ranch at San Antonio de Areco. He studied law, which he never practiced. He traveled extensively in Europe, knew English literature well, and was as familiar with French as with Spanish. He was one of the initiators of the post-World War I literary movement in Argentina and a co-founder of the literary reviews *Martín Fierro* and *Proa,* in which the early work of many of the young writers who later achieved distinction first appeared. A rare synthesis of Europe and America had been effected in him. He was not a mere tourist or traveler in Europe. He spent long periods there, especially in France, where he had a host of friends. But always the memory of his homeland, of his ranch on the pampa, was uppermost in his thoughts, and when he wrote, it was the scenes, the people, the emotions of that life which he loved and carried within him that he brought to his work. In a letter to his friend the French writer Valery Larbaud, whom he admired and for whose encouragement he was very grateful (but whose influence on him has been much exaggerated), he said in 1926, when he had finished *Don Segundo Sombra:* "Don Segundo has, among other intentions, that of establishing my claim to the title of literary disciple of the gaucho. I recognize the influences writers whom I admire have exerted on me, and I have no intention of denying them, but I feel that this act of justice is called for. In me, because they were the earliest and most immediate, the narrations and dialogues I listened to with ineffaceable emotion as a child have been stronger than the amplifications of thought and, above all, of expression which these emotions have undergone by reason of my cultural formation. I am afraid that I am not expressing myself clearly. First there is the seed, and even though in its development outward forces play their part, the vital principle of the tree it is to become is already present in the seed." The duality of Güiraldes's life, that of the traditional rancher of the pampa and that of the cultural emigré in Paris, achieved an equilibrium in which the one enhanced the other. And this equilibrium is reflected in his work, at one and the same time European and Argentinean, ultramodern and ultra-traditional, among the most original and enduring that Spanish America has produced in this century.

Güiraldes's first work was a volume of poems, *El cencerro de cristal* (1915), but it is as a novelist and short-story writer that he achieved his greatest originality, although the poet is present in everything he wrote. His first volume of short stories, *Cuentos de muerte y de sangre* (1915), is a collection of brief narrations, in many of which he evokes his country's past. They are told with a vividness, an economy, in which every word carries a maximum charge of emotion under the guise of apparent artlessness. *Rosaura* (1917), a short novel, is the delicate, moving account of a summer's love affair between a provincial town girl and a young man from Buenos Aires. Güiraldes handled this seemingly trite theme with deep tenderness. To the girl, Rosaura, this love was her life—and death; to the young man, a pleasant way to while away a vacation. In its descriptions, dialogue, and narrative quality *Rosaura* anticipates some of the best pages in *Don Segundo Sombra,* as is also the case with *Raucho* (1917), which is a kind of foreshadowing of the life that awaits the young protagonist of *Don Segundo Sombra* after he comes into his inheritance. *Xaimaca* (1923) is the sentimental diary of a traveler who visits many countries in the company of a beautiful, mysterious woman. This is the most European of Güiraldes's works; in it he employs all the vanguard techniques and brilliantly displays his abilities as a consummate artist. But it is in *Don Segundo Sombra* that he gives us the full measure of what he himself said the work of a Latin-American author must be: European techniques brought to bear on native materials. Within its simple framework is packed all the beauty of the land, of work, of the companionship of men, of freedom, of adventure, told in a language that is a blend of the precise, sober, yet colorful speech of the gaucho and Güiraldes's sensitive scintillating prose.

Don Segundo Sombra employs an old familiar literary device, that of the *Odyssey, Don Quixote,* the picaresque novels, to which it has a superficial resemblance, *Pilgrim's Progress,* and so many others: the peregrination. The boy sets out on the arduous enterprise of becoming a man. He realizes that everything he has learned in his shabby years as a mischievous town urchin, uncertain of himself or his origins, would stand him in small stead for his purpose. He needs a guide. "My life, it seemed to me, was bound to Don Segundo's, and although I saw the thousand hazards of it, I knew that I must follow him." Follow him he does, apprenticing himself to him, and when he had completed his Wanderjähre, he received his reward. But this was not recognition by his father, nor the fine ranch he inherited, nor the change in his social position. His reward was learning from the mentor he instinctively chose the art of living by gaucho canons: patience in the face of adversity, endurance, the vocation and pursuit of freedom, self-discipline, prudence, loyalty.

"*Don Segundo Sombra,*" writes Professor Ernesto Da-Cal, "is fundamentally a work of art. Art in the deepest sense of the word, that is to say the invention of realities whose truth is remitted to a different plane than that of living reality and superior to it. Abstraction and condensation of life, which, distilled by the alchemy of the artist, undergoes a transmutation into something far more valuable than the elements from which it comes. . . . The formula employed by Güiraldes—within his extreme originality—follows that of the great masters, Cervantes, Flaubert, Dostoyevsky. Perhaps this is what gives it . . . its unique place in the novel of Spanish America. Güiraldes has not channeled determined incidents of life toward his novel. . . . He has looked upon things and men, eschewing the temporal, the superficial, the ephemeral, seeking that fragment of eternity to be found in everything. It is a novel of pure Spanish stock—Cervantic—not only because of its composition, but because of its deep moral sense. There are those who, basing their judgement on formal aspects, would include this work in the picaresque genre, but this is a mistake: *Don Segundo Sombra,* from beginning to end, is an affirmation of faith in the positive values of the foundations, the historic and social origins of Argentina. Equally Spanish and Cervantic is the attainment of the plane of universal values through the employment of the peculiarly regional or national; thus, as in the case of *Don Quixote,* which being inalienably of La Mancha, of Castile, of Spain, can be accepted and understood by people of the most varied latitudes, so *Don Segundo Sombra,* Argentinian and of the pampa to the marrow of its bones, seems to all of us who belong to the Hispanic world to be our very own, even those who have never set foot in that country."

Leopoldo Lugones, the great poet and the outstanding figure of the generation which immediately preceded that of Güiraldes, had this to say of his literary art: ". . . it [*Don Segundo Sombra*] is a series of pictures without apparent continuity; but its unity, like that of life, which is the sum of a series of episodes, consists in living. And therein lies the secret of its irresistible appeal. Its interest lies in what is being lived, not in what the author narrates. This is the very desideratum of a work of art. There is nothing more difficult to achieve in writing, which is not a direct representation of Nature, as in the case of the plastic arts, nor does it arouse the emotions, as is the case with music. It can only evoke. Güiraldes possesses in the highest degree that gift whereby the writer reveals himself in his entirety with the natural synthesis of a bird in its song. To say of him that he painted the life of the country well because he knew it well, is to confuse the gift of painting with its instruments. He painted the country well, not because he knew it, but because he was an artist."

No study of Güiraldes, however summary, can be concluded without a word about the man as apart from the artist, although in his case there is a rare coincidence between the two. The values to which he gave expression in his creations were the norms by which he lived, less, perhaps, by deliberate choice than because they formed the essence of his being. Few persons can speak with greater authority on this subject than Victoria Ocampo, founder and editor of the literary review *Sur,* and an intimate friend of Güiraldes from childhood until his death. In an open letter published on the twenty-fifth anniversary of his death, she writes: "Moreover, to fully grasp your thought, your feelings (which were more important in you than your thought) one must know who you were. Only a part of you is to be found in your writings. Those who do not divine the rest read you only by half. This weakness (and it is a weakness, from the literary point of view, for a man to be of greater worth than his work) came from your human qualities: you squandered in living the gifts which others hoard for their art. . . . It is hard to love someone who gives himself wholly to his creations and puts into them the essence of his being. Save in rare cases, there is so little left of this someone outside his work. In your case it was difficult not to love you."

It is sad that Güiraldes's untimely death at the age of forty-seven should have brought to an end the career of this exceptionally talented writer from whom so much more could have been expected, as he had just come into the plenitude of his powers; but not because he had not left behind him a work that will live as long as Spanish is read, *Don Segundo Sombra.* It seems fitting that the final word should be said by his great friend and literary peer, Jorge Luis Borges: "The fatherland—if our hope and judgement prove prophetic—will continue to listen with delight to Don Segundo Sombra and everything connected with him. Ricardo, creator or chronicler of this hardy and endurant immortality, will belong to the ages, too. When this happens, when from the future ritual and taken for granted re-reading of *Don Segundo Sombra* . . . pious attention is turned to him who wrote it . . . this always axiomatic truth which today is paradoxical will once more be manifest: A man may be more than his work, the writer than the book. It will then be seen that Ricardo Güiraldes, the Argentine gentleman who seemed to live that form of unreality which the habit of wealth confers, took upon himself the stern purpose of being a saint, as those of us who lived close to him realized on more than one occasion. . . . It will become clear that not only mounted behind Don Segundo, his equestrian forbear, can Ricardo Güiraldes ride to immortality. It will be seen that God is no less infinite than His universe."

Harriet de Onís

SIGNET CLASSICS from Around the World

PLATERO AND I *by Juan Ramon Jiménez*

Translated by William H. and Mary M. Roberts with an Introduction by William H. Roberts. The delightful tale of a poet and his playful donkey by one of Spain's great Nobel Prize winning authors. (#CP302—60¢)

HEART OF DARKNESS and THE SECRET SHARER
by Joseph Conrad

Two tragic stories—one of a tragedy at sea, the other of a man's deterioration in an isolated trading post in the ivory country—by one of the world's greatest writers. Introduction by Albert J. Guerard. (#CD4—50¢)

BOULE DE SUIF and Selected Stories *by Guy de Maupassant*

A new collection of twenty-three short stories by the 19th century French master of this form. New translation by Andrew R. MacAndrew. Foreword by Edward D. Sullivan.

(#CD240—50¢)

THE RESTLESSNESS OF SHANTI ANDIA and Selected Stories
by Pio Baroja

Stories of adventurers, dreamers, and individualists by the Spanish writer, who, according to Hemingway, "Should have received the Nobel Prize." Translated with a Foreword by Anthony Kerrigan. (#CT149—75¢)

THE GOLDEN SERPENT *by Ciro Alegria*

The lyric story of the Indian farmers of the Peruvian Andes, whose livelihood depends on the turbulent Maranon River. Translated with Afterword by Harriet de Onis.

(#CP114—60¢)

AN OUTCAST OF THE ISLANDS *by Joseph Conrad*

Set in the tropical jungle of a South Sea island, the story of a white man whose career of treachery among the natives leads to final self-betrayal. Afterword by Thomas C. Moser.

(#CD239—50¢)

THE POEMS OF FRANCOIS VILLON

The strength and lyric beauty of Villon's poetry is recaptured in this brilliant new translation by poet Galway Kinnell.

(#CT288—75¢)